Ladies Who Knit for a Living

ILLINOIS SHORT FICTION

LADIES WHO KNIT
FOR A LIVING

Stories by

Anthony E. Stockanes

UNIVERSITY OF ILLINOIS PRESS

Urbana Chicago London

Publication of this work was supported in part by a grant from the Illinois Arts Council, a state agency.

"Ladies Who Knit for a Living," published in a slightly different form, *John O'Hara Journal,* 1980.
"Mr. Eustice," *Descant,* Summer, 1979.
"At the Border," *Chicago,* August, 1980.
"A Simple Dying," *Outerbridge,* Fall/Winter, 1980.
"Vandals," *Ascent,* Fall, 1976.
"75, " New England Review, Fall, 1979.
"A Simple Woman," *Sewanee Review,* Fall, 1979.
"The Milk-Glass Chicken," *Columbia,* Fall, 1978.

Library of Congress Cataloging in Publication Data

Stockanes, Anthony E., 1935-
    Ladies who knit for a living.

    (Illinois short fiction)
    Contents: Ladies who knit for a living—
Mr. Eustice—At the border—A simple dying—
[etc.]
    I. Title   II. Series.
PS3569.T596L3   813' .54   81-7421
ISBN O-252-00904-5 (cloth)   AACR2
ISBN O-252-00927-4 (paper)

For Harriet, for my mother, and for Julia Ann Rogers—because as Oliver LaFarge suggested, such debts cannot be paid, they can only be acknowledged.

Contents

Ladies Who Knit for a Living

Dover watches Lufkin gnaw at Thursday's second raspberry
bismarck. Tuesdays and Thursdays Lufkin always has two raspberry bismarcks. Dover: fascinated by Lufkin's routine just as he
sometimes marvels at his own invariable choice: I'll have (pause)
plain toast and (smaller pause, lower lip sucked, nibbled, a tiny
decisive hiss) black coffee please. And the waitress, celery-green
smock with carrot-orange pockets, orange insets on the sleeves,
orange piping on the lapels, stands with bony hip canted, pencil
poised over a small green pad with orange lettering. Between
"toast" and "coffee" she always pushes a frizzy comma of cement-
colored hair away from her eyes with her wrist. Then she always
says, "Juice?" Lufkin always shakes his head and Dover always
pretends to consider before he says, "No, not today. Just black coffee."

When his coffee comes, there is always a waxed paper cone of
milk on the saucer.

Dover wonders how these habits develop. What if one Tuesday or
Thursday one of them did something else, not a big something else,
just a minor change. Suppose Lufkin ordered two lemon bismarcks.
Or even a single raspberry. Suppose *he* ordered *buttered* toast. Suppose he held her hand between toast and coffee. What would happen? Nothing would happen, that's what. Everything would simply
stop, frozen. Habits, Dover thinks, are the gears of life. He believes
that is a line worth saving.

Lufkin is again telling him to fire Miss Kronopius. His napkin is a mess because Lufkin always tries to eat the entire jelly center at once and always lunges to trap raspberry snails leaking from his mouth. "A dizzy, Dover. A birdbrain. A dimbulb. If nothing else, that laugh—chapeep chapeep chapeep, like some kind of I don't know what. You can't keep your mind on business with that going on. A business is no place for chapeep chapeep. One of these day's it'll snap your brain." Worn teeth peek through a ruby film.

After ten years of mid-morning snacks they remain as they were at first meeting, Dover and Lufkin. It isn't conceivable he would call Lufkin "Jerry" or even "Gerald"; Lufkin would never call him "Martin." A city friendship, sustained more by proximity than preference. He knows Lufkin's office, one floor below his, as well as he knows his own, but Lufkin's home in Skokie is a mystery, a queer and expensive structure constructed for him entirely of Lufkin's complaints. They have exchanged comments on their wives but Kathryn and Carol are distant, intangible. And yet, if asked, Dover knows he would probably say Lufkin is his best friend. But if Lufkin died Dover wouldn't know about it. Sometimes the knowledge bothers him but he doesn't know what to do about it. He can't say, "Lufkin, if you die at home be sure and let me know." And could he carry a card or wear a bracelet like one of those medical alert things with: I Am A Dover. Please Contact My Best Friend Lufkin (No First Name) Somewhere In Skokie?

He watches Lufkin cram the doughy rind in his mouth and grind it to a lump of paste. "She's O.K."

Lufkin's throat sucks the wad below his tie knot. "No, not O.K. Very much not O.K. You can't tell her nothing, right? Listen, how many times have I been in your place—your place of *business,* Dover—and you tell her she's screwed something up, what does she do? Chapeep chapeep—aughh!"

Lufkin is only partially right. Miss Kronopius takes correction in a flippant way, with a tinkly laugh as though she doesn't care. But she never repeats her mistakes; the laugh is habit, not attitude.

"She's O.K." He doesn't say, "Lufkin, you have to be tolerant of people's habits. Besides, if I fire her as a secretary, how do I keep her as a mistress. This is a problem in employee relations."

Mild for late June, the heat pleasant. They take the long way back instead of cutting diagonally across the street. Lufkin on the outside as usual, they turn left, stroll a block south on Wacker, come back to Clark, turn north to Wells.

"So how's the missus?"

"Fine," Dover says. He seem himself in a store window, doesn't think he looks his age. In the window a mannikin models sportswear, cream slacks and a breath-soft blue sweater. Dover is tempted to come back in the afternoon. Where can he wear slacks like that? To Miss Kronopius's on a Thursday evening? Brush against anything, the dirt is going to show. And expensive! Seventy-five dollars for a pair of pants, that's crazy.

Dover knows he will come back.

Dover (again) imagines how it would be to have an exact duplicate of every bit of money he's ever handled. An inspired fantasy. Of course the serial numbers would show they were phony, but only two with the same number would never be noticed. The security of his dream is a comfort. Imagine, a perfect copy of every bit of money. Not just his own but every bill, every coin he ever held; change made at Griswold's when he was working Saturday mornings, the bank deposits for T & L, his first real job. Incredible, the money a man touched in his life. An immense pile of fives, towers of singles so tall you couldn't see the top, various loans taken out in crisp hundreds, mountain ranges of quarters, a dull brown ocean of pennies with here and there a new one glinting like sunlight. Just the dimes—a fantastic amount of money passes through a man's life. Suitcases full of money, black steamer cases full, closets so crammed the door would have to be braced by a chair. Dover never imagines doing anything with his treasure. Just having it again, all at once, what he once had, would be perfect. No strain of figuring out complicated deals, no translating numbers on a statement. Just to have it all back again in hard cash, to be surrounded by what he once had . . . a splendid vision.

Lately he has become more cautious, but it's much too late to save for his old age. While he was thinking of it as far off, hidden by a jumble of days, his old age came up and squatted on him. And "old age" isn't what it should be anyway. It isn't much different from "middle age" (he can't look back and see that as a definite period; it had no end, nobody rang a bell and said, "That's it, Dover, time's up. You're not middle-aged anymore. Now you're in your old age.") Old age isn't a different time, a time for relaxing, for sitting around on a bench by Buckingham Fountain feeding pigeons. It isn't anything. The big surprise is the lack of much change at all, in his life, in himself. You got some wrinkles when you were young, years later you had more wrinkles. Who could say this is an old wrinkle, but this little rascal here popped up when I got old. A wrinkle is a wrinkle. The only way to measure the time spent would be to have, all at once, every bit of money . . .

Once, on a mild day like this, walking the same route, he tried to tell Lufkin about the money, but he didn't know how to start. Casually, he asked Lufkin what he would pick if he could have anything he wanted. After Lufkin told him some mundane thing, he would tell Lufkin about the money. Lufkin would be impressed.

Lufkin bounced along with his penguin strut, toes angled out. For almost a block he didn't say anything and Dover thought Lufkin hadn't heard him. That was all right. It was a childish question.

Suddenly Lufkin stopped. "Anything? You mean just one thing, no matter what? Like maybe being invisible, something like that?"

People eddied around them. Dover was uncomfortable; he had never considered being invisible. "Something like that."

Lufkin's hands, speckled, hairy, had the sharp-tendoned delicacy of age. "I'll tell you . . ." He hunched over, locked the index finger of his left hand over the little finger of the right, waggled his arms. "Firestone's South Course. The 16th. 625 yards. A ball-buster. Nicklaus, one of the big bombers, somebody like that, just bogeyed it." He studied the imaginary ball with an intensity that made Dover see it, glaring white on the sidewalk. People flowed around them, impatient, amused, irritated. Two young men in vibrant shirts stopped to watch. "Two long wood shots and right in front of the green you got to pitch over." Heads ducked automatically to avoid the club head swinging back, cringed as the ball leaped away from the sweet solid "tock," arced in a sublimely smooth line above the trees, rolled to the pin. The two young men, a microcosmic gallery,

Lufkin's Legion, applauded. "I birdie it," Lufkin said with the only smile Dover ever saw on his face.

Dover didn't even know Lufkin played golf. After ten years.

They walked back to their building in silence. Dover remembers the scene often, the brief poignant exposure of a curious man's curious dream. His own seems sensible and insignificant and normal and petty compared with Lufkin's. He never told Lufkin about the money.

A depressingly small stack of mail, advertising flyers and bills, and Miss Kronopius's impersonal daytime smile welcome him.

"How's Mr. Lufkin?" The question another habit.

"Fine." He riffles the thin sheaf of call-back slips. "Billy say what he wanted?"

"Santiago's copy stands. You put a hold on them."

The Brothers Santiago never pay without a nudge. "O.K.," Dover says with depthless reluctance. "I'll give them a call."

He closes his door behind him. God, he is tired and it's only a little past ten. He does not want to press Santiago. Where does the money go? The office gobbles up so much, is so unnecessary. A mail-order business like this, who needs a fancy-shmancy office? A small space at the warehouse, a desk next to Billy's, would do. But the warehouse is in such a grubby neighborhood, two rented floors in a decaying brick building that stares at the river through grilled paneless windows. A man would simply rot inside if he had to go there every day.

He sits behind the desk and stares at the two black-and-white enlargements on the opposite wall. Both have a misty, nostalgic quality. Black-and-white is inaccurate; they are shifting blends of infinitely varied grays, insubstantial as smoke. On the left, a study of the city's skyline taken from a boat. He can remember the morning it was taken, the water immensely deep under the rented boat, the sounds of the city muted—not so much traffic then—the quiet slap of little waves, the rippled echoes of a tanker moving out beyond Navy Pier and close to shore the sail-less masts of the moored pleasure boats moving like windshield wipers across the buildings. The creaking of something, a buoy maybe. The most peaceful morning he had ever known. And such a long time ago.

The other picture shows—suggests—a bird, a winged shape at least, settling on a column or a piling or a stump. He can never remember when that one was taken; he found it on a roll of faces he'd snapped at random. Maybe it wasn't a bird at all, simply the face of a stranger blurred, transfigured by some freakish accident of the shutter. *Camera Yearbook* printed both of them. Somewhere he still had a dozen copies of the magazine unless Kathryn had thrown them out. The pictures had even been selected for the museum show that year.

He scrubs his eyelids with his fingertips. Such a long time ago. He was never sure whether they were actually that good or whether the titles Kathryn gave them, "The Death of Water" and "The Cruel Dove," were so opaque they gave the photographs an enhancing mystery. No matter what the reason, nothing else had ever been as good. Or at least nobody thought so. In a way, they were more Kathryn's pictures than his. Maybe not even hers. That was when she was reading Gibran all the time. No titles she suggested after that were ever as good, either.

"Santiago, you make me sick."

He was going to free-lance, be a regular artist with a camera, travel all over with Kathryn, maybe collaborate with Lowell Thomas. Brady, Atget, Eisenstadt and Dover. Portraits he didn't want to bother with he'd send over to Karsh, and Karsh would be grateful for the references. People would shuffle over to Bachrach when he turned them down. The slick magazines would say, "Get Dover. If not, we'll have to use that new guy, Avedon. But, Jesus, he's no Dover."

After the museum show the old *Sun* wanted him, but he turned them down. Well, he was still alive and kicking and the *Sun* was long gone.

The chair creaks protestingly as he swings around to watch the tiny slice of lake visible from the window. When he first rented the office the building had been one of the ten tallest in the city. Even then it wasn't cheap. But a great location.

I don't know (a dubious Kathryn). That's an awful lot of money. What if things don't work out . . .

Look, I can still work at my own stuff (Dover, a colossus, a magnificent impregnable shell of bravery enclosing the squirming worm of uncertainty) and run the business during the day.

Everyone was taking pictures, cameras were like radios, everybody had one and once you had a camera there were always a dozen gadgets you thought you needed. Buy cheap in wholesale lots and mail them out at a 60% mark-up. Like coining money, that's what Bern said, gently insinuating the pen into Dover's fingers. Believe me, if I didn't have this stomach I'd never sell. In a couple of years people would think of "Dover" like they thought of "Eastman."

If—no, when—they shoved up one more building he'd lose the last slender piece of lake. He hadn't used a camera in twenty years. Maybe he should bring one in, capture the lake before Rubeloff snatched it away forever. From here, a 50 mm lens. Use f/8 at 1/25 and maybe a #6 paper for contrast . . . Twenty years ago the sun would fill the room in the morning, lay wide trapezoids of creamy light on the carpet. Now he was in perpetual shadow.

Miss Kronopius buzzes him. Another habit, another useless expense. "I'm taking my break now." With only two of them in the office she could open the door and holler.

"Right. O.K."

"Did you call Santiago?"

"No, not yet." See, Lufkin? That's diplomacy. If I called someone her phone button would light up. "Miss Kronopius . . . "

"Yes, sir?" So formal. Somebody should be here to see how proper and dignified the office was run. Dignity—once you lost that, the whole thing was shot.

"I may go out this afternoon . . ."

"All right. Billy said Testrite is . . ."

"In case I don't get back before you leave, it's Thursday."

"Oh, I know that." You could tap the phone, who would find anything suspicious in that? Her laugh does sound like chapeep chapeep but Dover thinks it's pleasant.

His fingers know Santiago's number. Dover, you're sixty-eight years old! Why do they make you sweat like this? Where's the dignity? The voice that answers is different again. Santiago must have a harem. Which Mr. Santiago does he wish to speak with, please?

Paul. Oh, Mr. Paul Santiago is in Boston and isn't expected back
until the first. Luis. Oh, the voice is inexpressibly sorry; Mr. Luis
Santiago is in a meeting and *can*not be disturbed. May the voice take
a message? Is Leon in? Oh, the voice is devastatingly sorry, Mr.
LEE—own Santiago has just this very minute stepped out. May the
voice take a message, Mr. Grover? He leaves his name, angry and
relieved. He doesn't owe *Santiago* money, for chrissake, Santiago is
into *him,* so why should he be the one sweating? If he gave Testrite
the runaround . . . It's really a wonder the business has survived
this long, Dover tells the photographs on the opposite wall.

Right now, this very minute, he should be living quietly someplace. If he had taken the job with the *Sun* and if they had kept him
when they merged with the *Times,* he'd be three years retired. And
doing what? For one thing, drawing a little pension—that would be
a good thing, at least a little something steady coming in. Seventy-
five dollars for a pair of pants, another forty for the sweater. Well,
you couldn't get those on a skimpy little pension. So what do you
have now? The business, barely scratching along, a little in sav-
ings—very little because of Miss Kronopius, a lot less than Kathryn
thinks and someday *that's* going to blow up.

So let it blow up! Whose money was it anyway? Who sat in the
apartment all day and who came out every day, rain or shine? Who
was she to dump on him?

Years ago, when he thought things would always change and im-
prove, when old age wasn't real, was a phrase, an impossibility,
something that would eventually happen to somebody else, a different Dover, he was going to keep a record of Kathryn's faults.
Every time she pecked at him—and after he turned down the *Sun*
job she really started—about some piddley little thing, he couldn't
remember the countless things she did and he lost arguments simply
because he didn't have a good memory, because he was too tolerant,
overlooked too much. God, her memory was total then. Every
penny he spent, months later she remembered. Every word, every
little word, that might—just might, if you twisted it—be a criticism,
she tucked away and then, weeks later, brought them all out like
shish-kabob on the sword of her tongue. She probably even made
some of them up. She brought them out with such clarity, such

venom, it was only later, walking around trying to cool off, that he was certain he hadn't said them in the first place. But after patiently explaining what you meant, you couldn't go back and say you hadn't said them.

He should have started the file when he first thought of it, not put it off. He shouldn't have let himself be trapped into the undignified arguments. No, the thousands of flaws should have been saved, a neat record on index cards with the date and time and exactly what she said and did. That would have been the way to do it. A special shallow closet right over there beside the window. Three, four, sometimes ten a day, a precise inventory: the way she licked her spoon and stuck it in the sugar, the toothpaste tube strangled in the middle, lipstick on the water glass in the bathroom, matches around—never in—the wastebasket, books with pages dog-eared because she couldn't be bothered with the bookmarks he supplied by the pound, the radio turned down but not off so he was gradually conscious of a buzz like a mosquito and had to go looking for it, the times she put away a magazine he'd been reading, the way she . . . each one on its own index card, a permanent damning record stored in the closet, expanding every day like a potential avalanche building, snowflake by snowflake, while she picked at him for no reason. Maybe two closets, side by side, with a special wide door.

THEN—! after years of not saying anything, of perfect dignity, when she made the ultimate piddley carping remark he would silently bring her up here, lead her to the closet, point to it. And when she opened it the avalanche would come down, burying her in the astounding history of her intolerance. "See what you did to me," he would say with a resigned smile while only her toes poked out under the permanent damning indexed weight of her nagging. To have all her faults dumped on her, all at once . . .

Staying together, another habit? Maybe it was because he never kept the record and so never collected enough evidence to show her—or himself—what she had done.

Occasionally he takes Lake Shore Drive, audaciously going to his mistress right past his own building. Talk about expense. But it was a great location. You mentioned your address, people were impressed. This evening he rolls the window down and stutters his way leisurely through the traffic lights on Lincoln. A mistress at his age, that's something. Should have done it years ago. Of course, years ago there was no Miss Kronopius to delicately suggest it, but, if he looked, there probably would have been somebody. Who knew how many somebodies?

Through the afternoon the heat has accumulated, feeding on itself, collecting truck exhausts, tamping itself into the canyons formed by buildings. How could people live like that, no air conditioning, hanging out of windows hoping for a little breeze? And the shops! Mile after mile of grubby businesses. He was crazy to stick with it in a city where block after block after block of tiny stores shoved against each other, store-front restaurants, twenty lawyers to a block, fourth-floor podiatrists . . . crazy, all these people trying to gouge the same buck. What insane vision would drive someone to open the A & A Grill ("Today's Special—Beef Stew Homemade Pie") on the same seamy block that already held the Ace Restaurant, Corky's Grill, El Toro Taco Shop, Bonheur's Fine Foods, the Elite Cafe, Cavanaugh's Red Hots, the Food Hut, Maxine's Grill? One lousy block where the Tip-Top Grill, Berkowitz's Restaurant, the Eagle Eatery, the P & G Cafe and the Ace-High Cafeteria had died, the legend of their daily specials dead-white graffitti on plate glass, the interiors dark.

And porno movies! Oh, god, that was something else. How did they stay in business? Mob-money. Had to be. Some kind of tax gimmick. Any time you went in, what was there? Ten guys, a dozen? You couldn't dent the overhead on a dozen customers. In the Loop the big movie houses were crying and they had a hundred times the business.

Block after block of it, a regular Potemkin village. It wasn't surprising that so many died; what amazed was the survival of so many, the new ones endlessly opening where so many had failed. So who are you to wonder, Dover? You could look in the yellow pages, that would scare you silly. Start with Photo Color Prints, go through Photo Finishing Retail, finish up with Photoprints, there were thirteen pages! Everything from International Camera Corp's big ad (a ball-buster, Lufkin would say, an ad that size) to Level Optical's skimpy single line. His own modest two-inch, column-wide ridiculously expensive notice lost in the confusion of page 1088. A crazy world. Why stick with it? Why not just sell out? To whom, Dover? Are you going to hold your stomach like Bern and grab somebody off the street? No problem. There's always somebody with a positive lust to get wedged into those thirteen anonymous pages.

So, sell.

And then what?

A horn behind him brays a warning and he lurches forward. In the rear view mirror he watches the cabbie's mouth form words.

And then what? For one thing, get out of the city. Who needs air like the inside of a vacuum cleaner bag, a thirty-minute hunt every time you want a parking place, fruit that looks good on the outside and tastes like paper, gum on your shoes all the time, tons of paper just drifting through the gutters . . .

The whole city is falling apart.

Used to be, you could drive through here or out on Irving Park or the south side, there were communities, real neighborhoods; Lithuanians, Poles on Division, even Swedes up around Belmont. Real little ethnic pockets. All that was gone now. Everywhere you looked it was blacks or Puerto Ricans or Mexicans—every other sign was in Spanish, for God's sake—or some kind of Indian running around in a turban. Half of Athens must be over here, there are so many Greeks. His cuff is grey, gritty. Perversely he leaves the window open, enjoying the city's decay.

Miss Kronopius lives on Wilson, the street here lined with trees that curve up in a cool arch, lay mottled, restless patterns on the pavement. The trees here have an air of permanence, not like those skimpy things strung out along Michigan, stuck in concrete like bare twigs. A few quiet brick apartment buildings between staid rows of narrow houses with porches; the houses hold themselves away from the sidewalk with steep wooden stairs. Residential, this is the way the city should be. But you go just a little back, around Broadway, and you might as well . . .

Miss Kronopius—Loretta now, after five o'clock, on Wilson rather than downtown—never automatically pushes the buzzer, makes him identify himself. He doesn't resent it. Not too much.

Better be safe than sorry with all the crazy things going on. Even here, under the cool, weathered trees, you're not that far from the craziness.

Just a few years ago I could take Kathryn for a drive up to Winnetka or maybe over to the Edgewater Beach and it was like being in the suburbs as soon as you got past North Avenue. Now the suburbs are out in Iowa someplace. You can't blame her for being careful.

Still, it would be better, more dignified, to simply press the buzzer and have the door open like he was welcome. Even better would be his own key, but he can see her thinking on that. Just for Thursdays, who needs a key? But since it's just on Thursdays he should be able to march right in without having to go through the rigmarole. Bending over to give his name to the speaker—did they expect only midgets to want to get in?

The whole business isn't what he anticipated. A little thing like getting in peels away his dignity: pushing the buzzer like a peddler, bending over, trying not to whisper "Martin" to her question—and too often she almost slips and says "Mr. Dover?" . . .

The stair light is out again and he has to feel his way. The stairwell smells musty.

You can tell this used to be a really good place. Little details, the pediment over the entrance, the grillwork around the speaker, those showed taste, somebody caring. Now it's just another place. And overpriced—one of these days Kathryn is going to find out about the beating the saving's taken this year.

He is breathing hard when he reaches the third floor. He leans against the wall, his shirt wet, listening to his harsh wheezing fill the space. He touches his chest. When you were sick, really sick, you got some attention, people excused things. People got annoyed if you were sickly, but they paid attention. Except for that once, he had never been sick in his life. But that once was wicked enough to count for something . . .

Kathryn didn't even get dressed, drove him madly through the twilight honking the horn like a crazy woman in her flannel robe.

He shakes his head, feeling his chest squeeze his lungs tightly, the rapid stutter of the pulse in his neck. That was something, all right. Racing through the streets with Kathryn holding the steering wheel like she was driving a fire truck and telling him to try to relax, it was going to be all right, he thought he was going to die. That was something.

The pain was such a surprise, so incredibly complete. A heart attack, you think it's going to be something in the left breast—in spite of the x-rays and everything he read about it later he still thinks of his heart as a plump, unattached valentine, literally heart-shaped, floating in the pericardium—but it isn't like that at all. It got you right in the stomach and spread like an explosion and you thought it was going to splinter your head.

"At your age you have to expect something like this, Mr. Dover," after they've put him in the room that cost an arm and a leg. What did a young shrimp like that know about what he should expect at his age? So many things he *had* expected never happened, who could say at fifty-five you can expect this, at sixty get ready for that? A heart attack—even a mild heart attack—was a serious thing, it *should* be a serious thing!—and it was always unexpected, no matter when it happened. Somebody keels over at thirty, everybody says, boy, that's terrible, such a young guy. Was it less terrible at fifty-five? Why should a few years change it from a tragedy to something you have to expect?

But he didn't mind dying, that wasn't it. In fact, he was actually disappointed when he didn't die, when they sent him home from the hospital with the brown plastic pill bottles, the mimeographed diet sheet, the pamphlet of instructions on exercises, the ache in his arms from all the shots and a bill big enough to run Evanston a month. Dying, that was something special, no matter when it happened. But coming home, *not* dying, *that* should be something special, too.

He'd only been disappointed.

What stunned was Kathryn's disappointment.

Not that she would have been happy to have him dead, that wasn't it. And she wasn't really *un*happy when he came home. It was just that—she'd adjusted to his dying. So quickly. It was a letdown for both of them and that she felt that way was something so immense he couldn't even accuse her of it.

Now, when he lifted something, she told him to be careful, but it was an automatic warning, without real concern, a mother saying, "don't put things in your mouth," but saying it out of habit, not really caring if the kid was sucking his thumb or cramming a Buick in his face. And it was funny because even though he was disappointed in not dying, he *was* careful, paused after climbing stairs, hesitated before picking up anything as light as a grocery bag, clenched his teeth in anticipation of the quick expanding total pain in the cavity under his breast bone.

What he dreaded most of all was that pain—that was really something—but there was also the pain of recovery, of coming out to find nobody but Kathryn knew he went in in the first place and she wasn't kicking up her heels when it turned out all right.

Occasionally there is a slight stinging sensation like an ice cube is being rubbed over the inside of his skin and he rubs his chest with slow, cautious fingers—feeling stupid doing it; you couldn't rub it away if it came and, if Kathryn notices, "Trouble?" (She is never more precise.)

"A touch of gas."

Sometimes there is no sensation at all and he isn't aware of his absently stroking fingers tracing the memory of the pain. Then her "Trouble?" is irritating. He automatically says it's gas. And she looks very slightly worried. (She doesn't drive now; sometimes he thinks her concern is the prospect of another tire-squealing horn-blaring race through the twilight to St. Luke's-Presbyterian. He takes secret painful delight in the knowledge that the hospital is no longer on Indiana and rigid in the blistering cocoon of his pain he would have to direct her, over to Congress.)

He never says, "Nothing," when she notices his unconscious stroking because it would end even her slight concern and that frightens him.

Miss Kronopius—Loretta—opens the door at his tap. It would be better if he came up to find her standing in the doorway, maybe with a drink in her hand, instead of waiting for his knock. It's better to be welcomed without having to bang the door. On the other hand, maybe it wouldn't be better. He needs a minute or two after the stairs to catch his breath. There's no dignity in showing up sweating and panting. He is warmed by this concern for his feelings.

But it would be nice if she was wearing something—well, something more mistressy instead of white knickers, white knee socks, wide red suspenders, white tennis shoes. To him they look like tennis shoes. Somewhere a rich fairy designer was laughing at these young women . . . not that Miss Kronopius was all *that* young; a young lady, but a *mature* young lady. She calls these ridiculous outfits her "home suits," something to relax in, completely different from the respectable, almost old-fashioned skirts and white blouses of the office. They're different all right. Knickers. Like some kind of old-time golfer. A swishy old-time golfer. He has a quick vision of Lufkin in her costume and smiles. She smiles a response.

He dumps himself in a chair shaped like a partially collapsed balloon, a crinkly black deflating ball, and continues to smile.

The knickers make a dry scratchy sound when she walks. "You look like you need a gin and tonic."

He is tired of his smile, wants to put it away some place, doesn't know what to do with it, has no replacement. "That sounds good."

God, this is an ugly room, the worst of the chaotic sixties preserved. Miss Kronopius takes *Apartment Life* and is drawn to the most hideous ideas in that catalog of hideous ideas. None of the furniture looks like furniture: barrels halved, covered with floral paper and glued to other barrels; two-by-fours, lacquered mauve and chartreuse, fastened together with chrome bolts; a throne-like object that was originally a wooden milk carton, two oak coat racks and yards of weathered awning. Red, green, yellow plastic boxes in a variety of sizes hold paperback books, artificial flowers. . . . Dover closes his eyes a moment. On one wall a huge poster advertises an ancient Ken Maynard movie. On the adjoining wall a square yard of sanded, black-spray-painted plywood flaunts four burnished hub-caps attached asymmetrically. The hub-caps are from Maxwell Street. Miss Kronopius—Loretta—calls it "found art" and it is her own creation; in *Apartment Life* the plywood was painted a duller black. Dover remembers when Maxwell Street was really a place to go for bargains, when the words hanging in the air were plaintive *meshuggaas* and *fahtumult,* a kind of wailing poetry, instead of strident repetitions of "mothahfuckah," when gypsies knocked on plate glass windows to lure young men in for palm readings and, inside, invited-tugged young men into humid back rooms for more intimate palmings.

A year ago he considered moving his collection of Auchincloss to Wilson Avenue, to establish himself in this sanctuary. At fantastic expense he had everything Auchincloss wrote bound in moss-green Morocco leather with gilt stampings because he thought the man was an unappreciated genius. He gave the idea up; where would Louis fit in this jumble of beads and plastic?

From the tiny kitchen the tinkle of ice cubes soothes him; the kiss of glass and ice is light, summery, the sound of cool blue-green.

She sits with legs crossed on a platform of lumber and wire. "Martin, do you think you want to go to bed tonight?"

What kind of question is that? The basic idea of a mistress is you come up the stairs and you're made to feel dignified and reasonable and wanted and after some civilized conversation you go to bed.

And how can he answer? If it didn't happen like it was supposed to—up the stairs, torrid welcome (torrid welcome, but returned with dignity), a conversation about important, cultured things, into bed—what could you say? Like some kind of dirty old man, yes, I want to go to bed? Where's the dignity in that? Or, no, the idea never crossed my mind? How stupid. Did I spend forty minutes fighting traffic to come up here and sit on something that looks like a diseased bladder? Or, no, Loretta, I'm beat out from dragging myself up three flights of stairs so steep they should be against the law and I just want to sit here and feel the glass cool in my hand and my only desire is that my heart should quit threatening to race away my time like a crazy taxi meter? I just want to sit here and not move, not smile . . . could he say that?

"Why?" he says cautiously, unable to find an answer.

"My period started this afternoon." She smiles brightly and drains half her glass, wrinkling her nose at him over the rim.

He is relieved. And disappointed. And sad. He doesn't want to go to bed at all, has dreaded it. It's been a nagging threat in the back of his mind. But, after all, when you're paying for a mistress, even a one-day-a-week mistress, there's an obligation, a disappointment when things don't work out as they should. And he is saddened, not only by her menstruation—mistresses did it just like wives; it just wasn't something you considered—but by her language. Kathryn would never come right out and say "period" like that. "It's that time of month," that was graphic enough when Kathryn still had the problem and there was a wealth of unspoken detail in the varied inflections she gave *that*. In some ways Loretta was not quite the lady Miss Kronopius was. Miss Kronopius went to the ladies' room during the day; but on Thursday evenings Loretta went to the toilet . . .

This is the fourth Thursday in a row nothing's happened. Well, that's not quite true. So they didn't go into the bedroom with the weird copper-finned contraption dangling from the ceiling, the octagon of stained glass suspended in front of the window. He can sit back, relax—as much as he can relax in the odd chair—and talk. That's not a bad thing. Maybe it's better than flopping around. Miss Kron—Loretta—is a good listener, sometimes a super listener. It's a good thing, having someone young listen to you, be interested in what you're saying. Like keeping a diary. Only better.

The witty epigrams: "Loretta", looking through the glass into the distance with a slight smile . . . more of a half-smile, really, wry, experienced, "Loretta, marriage is an education. It has its own three r's: romance, resentment, routine." Getting that just right, arranging it so it seemed to come out spontaneously, the sudden bloom of wisdom on the stalk of a sophisticated life, took some practice. In fact he'd driven past Wilson all the way up to Peterson working on it. But it was worth polishing because now it was locked away in her head.

Years from now Miss—Loretta—would be married. Or maybe she wouldn't be married; an old lady, maybe, who'd look back through the years to the precious, exquisitely brief Martin Dover time and tell her companion (someone; at times he imagined a grandchild, but that complicated things. More likely, a dewy-cheeked young girl who looked up to Miss Kronopius): "My child, years ago a very wise friend"—she'd smile at that, a secret wistful smile for the "friend"—"once told me something I've always remembered." A pleasant thought, the knowledge his precise sentences would be lovingly passed on, held gently and examined, gaining lustre with the retelling. When he imagines it he gives her per-

fectly coiffed white hair and dresses her in a version of her office
uniform; knickers don't fit the picture.

He can tell her things and she pays attention. He makes her know
what it is to be young when Chicago was a different city, when West
63rd was a world apart from the Loop, when the most delightfully
foreign treat was a can of peaches stolen from the topmost shelf of
the towering white cabinet on the back landing and eaten warm in
the secret cave formed by sunflowers bobbing on scratchy green legs
behind the garage.

She is very good at paying attention to the thoughts he discovers,
the memories he finds stacked away in dim corners of his mind, their
colors amazingly fresh when he brings them out.

"You know," he mused once, "It's really hard to figure out just
who you are. Not you personally. I mean everybody 'you.' "

"Oh, you know who you are." When she yawns her face is very
young. Dover vows to bring a camera to capture the sleepy innocence of that expression.

"No, really. For example, my father died when he was thirty-
five— "

"That's too bad."

" —and I can remember him as being—oh, what kind of man?
An old guy. That's something, eh? Imagine, an old guy at thirty-
five. I was ten years old, to me thirty-five was as old as you could be.
And big. So now I'm *almost* thirty years older than he was when he
died, but I still think about him as being so much older than I
am . . . it's a strange feeling."

"I imagine."

A mistress is a wonderful thing. You can tell her what's on your
mind and she sits and listens, doesn't just sew and nod without
really paying attention.

"Lufkin said a very interesting thing to me today." He never
mentions Lufkin's attitude toward her; he can't discuss her with
Lufkin, but tries to share Lufkin with her. "I've been thinking
about it all afternoon. He said—I don't know what we were talking
about, it doesn't matter—but he said his father once told him there
are only two kinds of people in this world. One kind is ladies who
knit for a living. Isn't that a great line? It's so—so quiet, so com-

plete, you get the whole idea—bang, just like that. Just sitting there your whole life, just knitting away, miles and miles of yarn strung out behind you, never finishing anything, just knitting away, spending day after day . . . "

"I don't think people knit much anymore." Two triangles of tiny creases touch the corners of her eyes when she frowns. "A lot of people do crewel though. That's really in. I've got a friend who works at the Merchandise Mart—she's really an actress— " her eyelashes flutter like little wire brushes when she's excited and she leans forward with her shoulders pulled back. To Dover she is the figure on a ship's prow. "She got called back once for an audition at Second City, but she was too tall. She does crewel all the time. She says it helps her relax. She's got cushions all over, on all her chairs. All the cushions have dogs' heads. Or lions. Her whole place looks like it's full of animals."

Dover sighs. "That's not really what I mean. 'Ladies' aren't just ladies, it's men, too. Everybody. And knitting is—you know— "

Loretta prowls her friend's creweled apartment. "It's really great for her because she's crazy about animals but she can't keep pets. She's allergic."

"That's too bad."

"What's the other one?"

Dover often finds the disconcerting flit from topic to topic delightful. Often, but not always. "Other what?"

"You said Mr. Lufkin said his father said there were two kinds of people. What's the other kind?"

Dover is nonplussed. "Isn't that strange? I don't remember. I don't think he said. Maybe it's not important."

"Mr. Lufkin is very strange."

Dover surrenders glass. Sighs. Wishes this were a more traditional arrangement. A mistress is a wonderful thing to have, but Thursdays only . . . still, those are her terms. And she will not quit her job. These days a woman has to have her career, Loretta says with animation. Dover doesn't insist. Maintaining her full time would be economically devastating. The weekly envelope he never quite feels comfortable leaving on the plexiglass-and-sewer-tile table are drain enough as it is.

Driving home along the lake he thinks it is a very satisfactory arrangement, all things considered. But sometimes he studies his satisfied dissatisfaction. It would be better to have a mistress he could visit when the mood struck him, someone breathlessly waiting no matter when he arrived . . . but then, the mood doesn't come that often. Between Miss Kronopius's exuberantly healthy embrace and Kathryn's last phlegmatic grunting there is an enormous span.

The first time in Miss—Loretta's apartment was almost like being with the mustached gypsy on Maxwell Street. Except instead of being too quick he was too slow. Nothing happened. Not that it was anything to be ashamed of, those things happened, even to young men. But he'd felt so damned helpless, so—undignified. Lying there, watching her fingers work, all those turquoise rings chilling him, puckering his flesh into a soft stubborn curl, he didn't know what to do with his own hands, found himself patting her shoulder. He'd spent the whole day imagining how it would be, how her little gasps would sound (they would sound, he imagined, just like Kathryn's had sounded during the early years, soft explosions in her throat, an accelerating breathiness, almost laughter, almost weeping), even had to adjust his trousers around the unfamiliar tightness when he envisioned her without the oddly exciting plain white blouse. She touched his chest with cold ring-wrapped fingers. "That's all right, Mr. Dover . . . "

"Martin."

" . . . sometimes it happens that way. You're probably working too hard. Next time you'll probably come three times." Her skin picked out glowing light points from the glass suspended in front of the window. In the cool blue twilight she had been a soft statue, a Venus. It had been years, scores of years, since Kathryn could sit like that, her legs tucked under her.

When Dover remembers the first time he thinks of Kathryn and when he remembers his hand on Loretta's blue smoothness he shudders involuntarily.

Nothing is quite as it should be, is faintly blurred at the edges. Just a little out of focus. It would be nice to have a mistress waiting for him all the time; but he doesn't mind *not* being expected to pop up at odd times. No matter which way you look at it, it's O.K., and, as Lufkin would say, not O.K.

Dover devises a plan after that first failure. He leaves the office early on Thursdays and goes to a pornographic movie on Clark for preliminary stimulation. He is surprised at how expensive it is. He has to go all the way out to Lawrence to find a theater that charges less than two dollars and that's too much trouble. Eventually he settles on a Lincoln Avenue movie; it's convenient and it advertises 16 mm films. Dover equates this with amateurs—God knows, there are a lot of amateurs taking sexy pictures. You can tell that by some of the handwritten questions in the mail—and he thinks watching amateurs will be more exciting than watching professionals. For a while, a matter of weeks, his plan works fairly well. When he is in the apartment on Wilson he closes his eyes and remembers the movies. Loretta, knees tight against his ribs, rides him with a massaging action she says is very exciting. Dover is wordlessly grateful to her.

But the movies become boring.

The stories never change.

The men are usually the same and Dover cannot empathize.

The performances are professional and the camerawork is hopelessly amateurish.

He continues to visit the movie on Thursday, locked into yet another habit, but often he dozes after the performers take their clothes off. Awake, he finds himself concentrating on odd details: the men never wear shorts. Don't their trousers chafe? So many of the performers have bad teeth. Not rotten, just yellowish, uncared-for; the close-ups of mouths seem to be shot through beige gelatin filters. And there are so many blemishes, so many pimples, especially on buttocks. Dover returns to the street unrefreshed by his nap.

He took Miss—Loretta—to watch C. J. Lang (after a number of critical viewings he thought she looked, dressed, quite a lot like Loretta) to see what her reaction would be, to see if she would identify with—and perhaps imitate—Miss Lang. As far as he could tell she didn't have much of a reaction.

"What did you think about it?" He never suggested Loretta do anything like that and she never volunteered.

"It was O.K.," she said and there was such a lack of anything in her voice he didn't know how to interpret it. "What about you?"

"It was O.K.," he says carelessly. He took her to an Armenian restaurant and she was enthusiastic about that. Dover envied her appetite.

He parks in the basement garage, but instead of taking the elevator he wanders back outside, walks to the corner, walks across the street to the lake. A gentle wind moves the water with the heavy caressing sound of Miss Kronopius's thighs brushing when she wears the scarlet velvet trousers. Looking down he sees the jumbled footprints in the sand as though he is above a cratered desert. There is a strong smell of decaying alewives from the beach. For a long time he stands against the railing watching the boat lights moving far out beyond the breakwater.

He should sell out, that would be the smart thing. If he doesn't, there is no telling what will happen. Or specialize. Now that's an idea. Get a really hot salesman, take on just a few lines as an exclusive manufacturer's rep and concentrate on those. It's not too late to start something. All these years, he should have some kind of reputation . . . business is going to hell, little by little. A sudden drop, that's one thing. But the chipping away, that's worse. There are so many Santiagos now.

Tires hiss on the pavement behind him.

Things are in bad shape, there's no use denying that. He rubs his hands on the scaly railing, wonders why he feels no panic. There have been so many moments of crisis, bills not only unpaid but unpayable, he's been almost desperate enough to visit a couple of doctors for sleeping prescriptions. Somehow, while he planned on how many pills he'd need, things worked out, even when he was sure they never would. But things never *stayed* worked out.

He has not—yet—told Miss Kronopius this. The truth begs for the proper setting: it would be nice if she had an apartment with decent furniture. And a fireplace. Definitely a fireplace. It would be good to lean against a fireplace mantel with a glass in his hand. Brandy. Or an expensive port. Things you said had more—dignity—when you could lean against something, one hand in your pocket.

"It's something you learn with time, Loretta. You're much too young yet . . . " she would pull her lips together in a soft negatory cave. "No, I mean it. Only with time." He moves his glass in little circles, reflects. "You learn that all your life you're in tight spots and sometimes you think you'll lose your mind. It's very bad and then, for a while, it gets easier, but once it's been bad you never really relax because you know it's going to be bad again. Finally, one day you're in the same tight spot you were in originally and you think nothing's changed and nothing's ever going to change except you suddenly realize you're not desperate this time, you accept it as natural and you figure, what the hell, it'll work out again. And it does. Oh, sometimes you wake up thinking, 'Not *this* time, not this time!' and you want to jump out of bed and just run around the room, beating your head against the wall. But you don't. You just go back to sleep."

He must polish it, reduce it to a few sentences at once stunningly simple and faceted as a diamond so that she can store it away because it's important she get it right.

"Dover, I'm asking for a favor."

Dover's stomach contracts. The coffee shop turns dark and ominous. Lufkin is going to destroy their friendship, touch him for a loan that, even if promptly repaid, will alter their relationship in a terrible way. Lufkin, don't bring money between us! "Lufkin, business is so bad right now— " in the moment of panic he realizes he sounds like Lufkin, his voice too high, the words chopped off, the phrases Lufkinish. He takes a deep breath. "Lufkin, I got an inventory that just sits there like it's nailed to the floor. Billy, my warehouseman, tells me ten times a day— " the words a roar of despair, torn from the pain in his chest.

Lufkin watches him warily. "Dover, don't be such an ass."

"I thought you wanted . . . "

"I thought you wanted—aaghh." Disgustedly, Lufkin waves a shred of Friday cinnamon doughnut. "I said a favor, a personal thing. I need money, you think I got to go to strangers? Aaghh. Listen, what I want from you, I want you should change with me. You take Wednesdays, give me Thursdays."

Dover is conscious of a huge swelling emptiness, the hungry feeling he had coming home to Kathryn's lack of joy. "Are you telling . . ."

"Wednesdays are a bitch for me. The only nights I got free are Mondays and Thursdays. And Sid Hampshire, that bazoola, won't budge on Mondays."

Dover spreads his hands, embraces the celery green and carrot orange of the coffee shop. "Sid Hampshire? From Busnell Reality, that Sid Hampshire?"

"A bazoola, that one. Dover, is it going to kill you, changing one day?"

"Miss Kronopius?"

"So what do you say?"

"Miss Kronopius? Lufkin—Lufkin, you keep telling me to fire her! Chapeep chapeep chapeep!"

Delicately Lufkin pats sugar grains from his mouth. "Dover, what's that got to do with anything? That's business. In a business, she's terrible. You can't run a business with her around."

Dover wonders why he doesn't feel sillier, why this queer betrayal does not destroy him. He sees his Thursday afternoons, free of porno movies and the Everest of stairs, stretching out endlessly.

"Lufkin, let me think about it. Maybe I should get out of the gypsy business."

Lufkin blinks with saurian disgust, his "aaughh" a soft belch.

Kathryn is watching television. At least the television is on. She doesn't seem to be paying attention. Her fingers work the seam of the tent-like slip she is repairing. She is always sewing something. How much time does she spend stitching rips in her clothes? She is really a thrifty woman.

"You're home early."

Dover shrugs. All of his muscles have weights attached. "One of those days. What law says I have to work til midnight every Friday?" It is almost ten o'clock. He looks around the apartment. He spends very little time here. Except for Auchincloss, a cold green rectangle, there is very little of him in the room. Kathryn's long-dead sister squints at him from a photograph on the mantel.

"I've been thinking. Maybe I should sell the business." He sits down gingerly, aware of throbbing aches in his thighs and shins.

"And do what?" She doesn't sound curious.

"I don't know. Maybe we could get a small place somewhere. Maybe move to Arizona."

"Arizona." Her teeth worry a piece of thread. "We don't know anybody in Arizona."

Where are they, the people they'd known, called friends. Lufkin, there is limitless cruelty in your "strangers." "We don't know anybody here."

Her teeth, the second set, look strong enough to bite through steel. "I know Lena, Sandy Pressman, Alice, Steffie, the Brookmeyers, Juanita Paulikas . . . "

Who are these strange people? The names sound familiar, road signs glimpsed briefly on a drive long ago, a litany of out-of-the-way places.

"Lena who?"

A commercial pulls her eyes up. "Lena is Lena. Lena in 27B Lena."

Dover recognizes the name as he recognizes but cannot identify certain smells. It is tantalizingly familiar.

Dover lets a minute, then another stretch themselves out. His belly and brain conspire in ineffable yearning.

"Kathryn . . . "

She wags her head at the television. "That's so stupid. Who cleans a bathroom in a dress like that? Why do they let them put that junk on?"

"Kathryn . . . "

"Mmmmmm?"

He brings it to her from a great distance, offers it as a rare and precious gift borne across unmapped places. "Kathryn, do you want to go to bed?"

Her head moves so slowly he thinks he can hear her neck bones creak. "No, of course not." She blinks at him in mild surprise across a grey wash of years. "Do you?"

He thinks about it, seriously thinks about it. "No, what I'd like is some peaches. Right out of the can."

"Well, be careful you don't spill."

"We've got canned peaches?" It is a discovery of shimmering beauty.

"In the cupboard over the sink. Next to the green beans. Be careful you don't spill."

The muscle weights loosen. He smiles contentedly, but he doesn't get up. He talks to her, slowly at first and then, leaning forward, he strings words together in brilliant beaded strands and flings them in her lap. Occasionally she shakes her head at the television and mutters something. He tells her about Santiago, a hundred Santiagos, about Lufkin—what he knows or suspects about Lufkin—about the senseless sublime efforts of people to open new food shops all over the city. Without planning to, but working toward it inevitably, he starts to tell her about Miss Kronopius. He notices she has gone to sleep, mouth open, teeth slightly parted. She looks so old, so completely defenseless. He squirms back in the chair and tells her about Miss Kronopius anyway.

Her dry snores vibrate in the silence when he lowers the television sound. He brings a can of peaches into the living room and eats them slowly, being very careful not to spill. He goes back for another can and watches television without seeing it until the station signs off.

Mr. Eustice

Familiar sights: from a distance, the town water tower, a squat silver
spider on spindley legs; closer, St. Procopius, the lightning rodded
steeples of the Weddersons (a sprawl she laughingly pointed out as
early Charles Addams—and, with a secret shiver, called Gothic),
the rough vaulted arch of elms when they turned into the street.
These relaxed her. Even the seep of rain a comfort now.

Connie hugged her, offered her cheek to Earl. "How was the
trip?" Before she could say all right, Hillary said, "Jo-Jo got sick
all over," and Joel said, "She got sick worse. On the door," and
Earl said, "What a push. And a puke stop every ten minutes. I said
we should stuff 'em full of dramamine before we started. Didn't I
say that, hon?)" Connie clucked sympathetically and squeezed her
waist.

The living room compressed and molded her mood, a sense of
relief, of a return to something calm, secure. There were some
changes, there always were, and she catalogued them with mingled
regret and pleasure. The walnut drop-leaf table in the hall under the
gilt-framed oval mirror was new, the occasional chair beside the bay
window was now covered in tan corduroy instead of lemony velvet.
But the changes only intensified the impression of permanence.
Even this year's palm fronds, bleached and brittle, twisted in a long
loop behind the bronze and ivory crucifix, were exactly right. Their
shadow was a precise memory.

She kicked off her sandals and collapsed on the sofa, tucking her
feet under her. Connie lit a cigarette. She looked thinner. Earl

tramped upstairs with the luggage, the children at his heels. Joel
fretfully told his sister not to push.

Sharon thought her sister looked tired. "How's dad?"

"Sleeping. He had a bad night."

Sharon nodded. There wasn't anything she could say to that.
Each time they came—and the postcards and letters between visits
carried the same message—his nights were bad. It no longer had
meaning, stirred no alarm. He slept poorly at night, but dozed during the day so it equalled out. She smelled a faint medicinal odor
over the flowers Connie kept in various pots and Connie's scent.
Connie did overdo the cologne (Hillary, in the car, asked if she
would have to sleep with Aunt Connie. "She smells funny." Sharon
hadn't denied it; she said Aunt Connie smelled nice, not funny. Like
lavender). "I won't bother him now." She was ravenously hungry.
"I thought Joe and Frannie would beat us in."

"They got in about an hour ago. Joe was out of cigars and Frannie needed some things."

"Frannie always needs 'some things.' "

Connie's laughter quick, brief. "Anyway, they went over to the
Super V."

Sharon wrinkled her nose. Her hands smelled of the children's
vomit. "Hey, I'm glad to be home."

In the familiar bathroom she let the water run after she dried her
hands, wondering if the smell was her imagination or whether the
lingering odor was in her clothes. She put the toilet seat cover down
and sat on it, willing the cramps to start. The pill was effective, she
insisted again, straining for confidence. 99% effective; she'd read
that somewhere. But it was late, much too late, and that nagging 1%
made her head ache. She pushed the list through her mind: the strain
of getting things ready for the trip, the trip itself, the dozen and one
annoying little worries that formed her daily routine and might have
knocked her system out of kilter. She made them do their bobbing
carousel and felt better. With a few days to relax now, it would
probably start.

"Isn't this weather something? We had drizzle most of the way. A couple of times I even had to hold it down to the limit." She thought again how much Joe looked like his father, how similar their voices were as Joe got older. "Back home we've already had more rain than we usually get in a year." Even his hand, waving the cigar and tracing hazy blue-grey designs, was like his father's, long and pale. Why didn't he ever tan? And he was developing the Holt pouches under the jaw.

She heard Connie clanging pans in the kitchen and tried to ignore it. She didn't want to leave the sofa. "Connie? Can I give you a hand?" Her sister said no, it was no trouble, she wasn't fixing anything fancy. Sharon relaxed. Later on, when things settled down, she'd clean up the dishes and let Connie take it easy. She felt a surge of affection. Later on, when things settled down, they'd have a long talk. There was so much she wanted to say.

Earl scrubbed his scalp, yawned. "Got to be a record, this rain. Next time we're going to make it a two-day trip. Getting up at three, ramming it like crazy to make it in one day—too much." Sharon knew he would now say, with weary pride, exactly how far he'd driven. "Eight hundred and three miles, right on the button, our door to here."

"Doesn't Shar spell you?" from Frannie, petite and incredibly unrumpled in a simple frock that shrieked "expensive." Even with Frannie's discount, Sharon knew it cost twice as much as anything she had, even the Talbot's burgundy knit.

"Nah." Earl winked at her and Sharon smiled back wanly, knowing what he was going to say; now she always knew exactly what he was going to say. "We made this deal. I drive and she cleans up after the kids' whoopsies. I took the easy part." That made her feel so— so dowdy, something out of Erma Bombeck. Why mention the kids' car-sickness? Wasn't there some achievement to mention? And the euphemisms—"upchuck" and "ummy-tumbles" and "whoop-sies"—were so excessively cute they sounded obscene. Earl grinned at Frannie. "You two jet-setters couldn't wedge a kid into that bomb of yours." Sharon winced. Mention of kids around Frannie seemed cruel. But somehow, Earl could lumber through the most delicate subjects and no one minded. "What kind of mileage you getting, Joe? About two to a gallon. Downhill?"

Was the envious note in his voice when he talked about Joe's sporty little car obvious to the others or was that curdled note something she alone picked up? The cigar smoke, now that Earl was smoking too, formed a gauzey false ceiling and made her blink. What if the period didn't start?

Frannie patted her husband's arm. "Careful, honey, he's trying to set you up. End of the year and he's sitting on a lot full of schlock four-doors getting rusty." She stuck her tongue out at Earl, erasing the sting, and his face twisted into an exaggerated injured innocence.

Joe—how familiar the gesture was—stroked his nose. "That's right, Earl? Boss on you to move some clunkers?" Frannie giggled.

"Oh, oh, oh, a knife in the heart. Right in the goddamn aorta, babe! Hey, but listen now, now that you mention it—" he overrode their groans, "I mean, seriously now, I can get you a sweet deal on a four-door. Clean. Really clean. Full power, the works." He moved his hands, creating a smoky halo around his head. "Would you believe it, this week only, I've got this special—no, *super* special 'brother-in-law-named-Joe' discount. Took a special clearance by Detroit, right from the top." He parodied the sly car dealer, voice viscous, "Nothing down, a year's free car washes, and I zip over to keep the old lady company when you're out of town . . ."

Joe's laughter, a shrill whinny so much like his father's—as his father's used to be—cut him off. "No sale! No way! Right above our bed we've got this little plaque, 'Beware of Minnesota Car Dealers.' We read it out loud every night. Right, Fran?"

"That's right." Her face solemn, pinch-cheeked. "Right after we say our night-night prayers. We say, 'Dear Lord, help Earl sell a lot of schlock cars—but not to us!'"

Sharon wanted to be alone in the house. No, not alone. Her father was part of it. And Connie, too. But just the three of them in the spacious quiet, her father in his chair and Connie moving in some distant room.

Joe studied the ash accumulating on his cigar, flesh lumping under his chin. His father's pose, especially with the bald spot spreading at the crown. "We may be getting rid of the Porsche. Or maybe Fran's MG— "

"Over my dead bod, sweetie!"

"—because we may be needing something more family size."

"Joe!" Frannie slaped his arm in mock outrage. "Honestly! Isn't he something? Was he always like this?" Sharon suspected the note of annoyance wasn't entirely feigned. "You!" Another stinging slap.

Sharon shifted, hoping the aching stiffness creeping out of her pelvis, radiating around her ribs, was more than travel fatique. "A chronic bean spiller. So tell us. We thought . . . " She didn't know how to phrase it, let her voice ebb away.

"Oh, no such luck." Frannie sighed, drummed the small hard mound of her stomach complacently. "All the little tubes are still dead ends. But we've been talking about adoption."

"Hey, that's great." Earl sounded sincere. "Hey, that's really great. It really is. Everybody should have kids. Right, hon? That's really great. So when do you take delivery?"

"Take delivery! Jesus, Earl . . . " Smoke sliding over the bald spot. "We're waiting for the new models. I'd like something in a seven-footer with racing stripes, eighteen with a slam-dunk and all ready to sign with the Hawks for a jillion so he can take care of his old man in his declining years. 'Take delivery.' Jesus, Earl."

"Actually, there's nothing definite." Frannie turned back to Sharon. "We're just kind of talking about it. Right now—well, financially— "

"Things'll straighten out." Joe sounded peeved, defensive. "Everybody's got the shorts now." He grinned at Sharon. "She doesn't want to quit her job, that's what bugging her. I told her, look at you. Lounge around the house, watch television, nibble chocolates, change a diaper now and then—can't beat that."

"I don't know," Earl haunched forward and she waited for his defense. "Our gross was down 7.02% last month over last year. That's seven point oh two and that's mucho hub caps. And last year was . . . "

She let them drift away. Earl looked so out of place in her father's chair, so—beefy. She had warned him about sitting there, but he always plunked down anyway, dwarfing the image of her father's bony sweatered shoulders. She pretended to listen, gnawed on the stupid cruelty of chocolates and diapers and, behind the mask, tiptoed away into herself, letting the security of the room, the whole house, flow over her. She took away the walnut table and the other additions, replaced them with the old, comfortable pieces. Was the Queen Anne chair with the leg Skipper chewed still up in the attic? Recovered and refinished . . . when she was Hillary's age, curled up in that chair, her father, glasses tilted up on his forehead, would . . .

Something thudded upstairs, followed by a keening moan. She hurried back, started to struggle out of the sofa.

"All right, knock it off up there!" Earl's voice trundled up the stairs. "Your grandpa's trying to sleep! Hon, you want to see what the hell's going on up there?"

Her toes chased a sandal under the sofa. Resentment a solid justified flare. Alone, she would have said, "Are *my* kids making a racket?" Frannie bounced up before she could frame something innocuous that would register her irritation.

"Oh, sit still, Shar. Aunt Frannie needs the practice."

"They'll settle down." She didn't want to go up, to say the familiar ineffective things, to hear: "he started it," "*she* started it first," "he pulled my . . . " She didn't want to have to react at all, didn't want to be embarrassed.

"Sure." Frannie patted her arm. "They're just normal kids. I'll just pop up anyway." Her bare tanned legs shuttered between the dark bulbous bannister spokes. They heard her, cheerfully gruff. "O.K., mob, here come de law . . . " The door closed on Hillary's dramatic recital slashed with Joel's squeekily fictitious innocence.

"Frannie loves kids. She's like ma was that way, Shar, you remember when you . . . " He began the long, demeaning story of Eddie Basher and her roller skates, a memory he shoved at Earl each year. And, each time, Earl laughed heavily at her foolishness, her mother's wry comments, turned to her to ask, "You did that? If Jo-Jo or Hillary pulled a stunt like that, you'd whale the beezers off . . . "

Connie in the doorway, hands wrapped in a dishcloth. "Anybody hungry?" Her sister's pose at once strange and familiar, she felt a rush of something painfully welcome.

"Buttermilk dumplings!" Her feet were swollen, resisted the sandals. She sniffed with delight; the aroma curled back to herself at ten, her mother lifting the cover on the blackened Dutch oven and blinking in steamy billows. Her father, sleeves neatly rolled up, at the head of the table—when did they replace the old spool-legged table?—and, on one side, their heads a descending age scale, Connie, herself, Joe. Her mother saying, "Anybody hungry?"

"Mmm, that smells great." Frannie had supervised a cursory washing and their faces were passably clean. "I told the monsters here," she hugged them and they pushed against her, "they could eat downstairs and watch TV. That O.K., Shar?"

Television was forbidden during meals. "Quietly," she warned and, aware of the carping note, purposely exaggerated it. Neither Hillary nor Joel looked concerned, frightened, or amused. They nodded automatically.

She had to trudge downstairs twice to tell them to keep the sound down. Hillary spilled milk on the old divan. While Sharon cleaned up the mess she could hear Earl's laughter from the kitchen; he laughed like someone pounding nails in hard wood, each "ha" sharp, solid, complete. By the time she returned to the kitchen, her food was cold. Later, tired by the trip, the kids were fretful and there was the expected but no less irritating fuss when they were ordered to bed. Joel complained because he had to sleep on the floor on an air mattress; Hillary complained because she couldn't sleep on the floor like Jo-Jo.

"Shar, why don't you let them stay up and watch TV a while. But Aunt Frannie," glowering fiercely and they giggled, "is solemnly promising you'll be quiet."

Of course they set up a chanting whiney "Can we, please, can we?" She felt witchy insisting they go to bed. She gave them two Nytols each, kissed their foreheads. Joel's face was slightly flushed, warm to her wrist. She gave him an aspirin, considered, broke another in two and gave that to him. She tucked the coverlet around his neck and turned down the covers on the bed. That 1% was real people.

In the kitchen the cold fluorescent light turned the leaves of the ivy crawling on the windowsill a dark oily blue. Frannie had changed into what Connie called "one of Frannie's Atlanta-chic outfits," a semitransparent ensemble of aqua and lace. Earl was obviously aware of the dark peaked smudges tipping her breasts.

"Get the natives settled?"

"Um. Had to give them a Nytol." Earl blinked at her. "I hate to do that, but tonight, with the trip and the excitement . . . "

"Two more victims for the drug culture."

"Joe!" Sharon found the constant arm-slapping an annoying affectation. "Can I duck up and kiss them nighty-night? God, I could just hug them to death." They were just dropping off, would be cranky, Joel had a slight fever . . . Frannie shushed her. "I'll be quiet as a mouse." Her slippers with dandelion fluff balls on the satin straps made sharp slap-slaps on the linoleum.

"Frannie loves kids," Joe said.

They sat over coffee; the conversation wandered lazily through half-formed sentences, the trite sweet memories of people long dead, frozen in comic poses. Connie rinsed the dishes, turning now and then to add a comment as she arranged plates in the dishwasher.

He came into the kitchen slowly, coughing, still using the aluminum cane with its four feet awkwardly after all this time. She kissed his cheek and he patted her shoulder, offered Earl a frail hand.

"You're looking good," Earl said.

Another cough, a mannerism. "Nights are bad." The bathrobe was too large now. There was a cigarette burn in one lapel. The ropey belt was frayed and, around the knot, discolored from his fingers.

"The kids wanted to say goodnight, but we thought you were sleeping."

"I heard them," he said and she didn't know if she should apologize. He went back to bed after a few minutes, slippers gliding flat against the floor, and they heard him trying to cough. For a while they kept their voices lowered.

"He doesn't look good," Joe said.

Earl yawned, stretched, the loose pale flesh under his arms jiggling. "No more of these one-day pushes. No way. Eight hundred and three miles, right on the button—that's pushing it too hard—" the last words spilling out of another yawn. "When you and Mr. Eustice setting up housekeeping, Connie?"

"Oh, any day now." Sharon thought Connie's laugh was forced. "He's been prowling under my window again, yowling like an old tom."

Even though it was a familiar response, Sharon smiled. The image of the severe Mr. Eustice crouched on the lawn, howling and rubbing his back against the pear tree, was a ludicrous delight. A widower for so many years he had reverted to "old bachelor," for as long as she could remember he was alone in the fussily neat brick house next door. She couldn't remember Mrs. Eustice at all, but she must have seen her years ago. Her memory of him was of a thin, unsmiling figure in crisp white shirt mowing the lawn. And his shoes were always shined. Whenever he was mentioned, her father always said, "He mows the lawn in a white shirt," packing the statement with disgusted awe, making it a summation. She couldn't remember when they began to kid Connie about him.

"Better grab him now, babe," Earl said and Joe nodded. "No matter what happens, you know an undertaker is going to work."

"Mortician," Connie corrected lightly and Sharon glanced at her.

" . . . and then, you've always got nice flowers around the house."

"Oh, Earl! That's gross!" Frannie pattered in, a swirl of scent and chilly blue-green cloth.

Joel slept on his back, the small white triangle of his face moist. She adjusted the cover under his chin and his gentle snoring stuttered. Earl's breathing was regular and heavy. This had been her room, and she missed the white, bow-fronted dresser, the wicker chair with its frilly skirt. Connie had replaced them with a sturdy oak six-drawer and a plain wooden rocker. She wondered if the white dresser was in the attic, the little chair's skirt grey and heavy with dust. Very faintly, she heard her father's cough. She could remember awakening to that sound—louder then because his room was at the end of the hall and he used the upstairs bathroom—and taking comfort in it: the predictable sequence of hacking, a subdued splash as he ran water over the cigarette and then the toilet flushing and the squeak of his door.

The bed (at least that hadn't been changed) was too narrow and Earl's weight sucked her into the trough in the center. She clung to the tilted edge. She was going to shake him, put a hand on the bare spongey fuzziness of his shoulder, but she took her hand away when he grunted. What would he say if she told him about the delay? He would somehow manage to make it her fault and then—the picture was so real she watched his eyebrows warp under the frown, the puckering of eyelids, watched his mouth form the words—he would say, "We just can't afford it," as if she had made a frivolous purchase and should march right back to return it.

She lay half over the side, knees drawn up under her chin, violently kneading her abdomen. Someone, years ago, in a whispered high school conversation, said that was the way to start a period. Beer helped, too. Unverified but stoutly maintained folk medicine. Another: a small bottle of ginger ale with a Contac in it, shaken up and used as a douche, an unfailing contraceptive. No one admitted trying it, but the formula was passed on with unquestioning faith.

She tiptoed downstairs. The refrigerator latch sounded very loud.

"Tapeworm kotchum Sharbabe?" She jumped. Connie, without makeup, her face much like her mother's now, slightly pudgy, yawned.

"I was looking for a beer. I thought I saw some in here earlier."

"I keep a few around for dad. He's not supposed to have them, but," a weary shrug, "he says they help him sleep. Maybe they do. It probably doesn't do that much harm." She eyed Sharon critically. "Beer on top of dumplings. Is that wise?"

Sharon straightened. The nightgown and robe made her look bloated. "Period's a little slow."

"Get the milk while you're rummaging around in there, will you? Cramps? You want a Darvon?"

Connie took glasses from the dishwasher and they sat at the table.

"No." She wanted to tell someone—but not Earl—about her worry, to ease the apprehension by sharing it. "I'd love to have a good case of cramps. Nothing's happening." She hesitated, waiting for the question, was disappointed when it didn't come.

The coughing, not habit now, dry and painful to hear, squeezed under his door. His bed creaked as he shifted his meager weight. His room had been a small enclosed porch, a combination greenhouse and catch-all room. Connie had it redone as his bedroom because of the light, the view of the yard and his trouble with stairs. And it was easier to take care of him down here.

Connie's wrist was dry and rough under her fingers. "I guess sometimes it's like trying to take care of a little kid, isn't it?"

"Um? Oh—sometimes. Kids don't tell you they're going to . . . " Connie's lips tightened. Whatever she was going to say hidden, a quick silent flash of something ugly.

"He doesn't look good at all." She thought Connie's answering shrug was callous.

"He's up and down. This week he's been restless. Maybe when the weather changes . . . "

"A few days of dry warm!" Connie smiled at that, mother's old prescription for summer moodiness, peaked plants, dad's grousing about the water seeping out of the sump in the basement. "A few days of dry warm," she would say placidly, "that's all we need." It became one of the family codes, a catch-phrase like "tapeworm kotchum Sharbabe," something with meaning beyond the words, a secret family slogan.

"Right. A few days of dry warm." Connie lit a cigarette. "The dampness really does bother his chest. He's been taking too much cortisone lately, but . . . " This time the shrug was resigned. Sharon sipped from the can and Connie said, "Use a glass," automatically.

"Yes, ma'am." She expected Connie to grin at the demure, little-girl response, but her sister didn't notice.

Connie traced wet designs on the table. "The weather's been vile.

Everyone seems to get down in the dumps after a while. The yard's a mess. I just haven't been able to get out there."

Sharon didn't want to talk about the weather. She wanted to tell Connie how she felt, to explain the fear that the period wasn't just late, that she dreaded another pregnancy, the inexpressible sensation of being less than real, merely an appendage of the swollen thing in front. And she dreaded the long months of cleaning up after the helpless thing, of never—it seemed such a small thing to want—of never having a room someone could come into without having to step over lumps of colored plastic and wood junk, the infinite ugliness kids spread, of wet stains on the sofa, of being forced to say, in that humiliatingly apologetic way, "Excuse the mess." Would Connie, here, moving through rooms never cluttered with rattles and blocks, understand any of that?

"I'm sorry if Earl gets on your nerves with the Eustice thing. I know it's probably not funny any more—I've told him, but, well, sometimes trying to get him to understand— " edging closer to it, she took a deep breath, waiting for the sympathetic, almost maternal, "I know. But you can talk to me, Shar."

"What do you think about George?" Connie watched her fingers move the milk glass in tight circles.

"George?"

"George Eustice."

"Oh. Oh . . . not much, I guess. He seems—nice. Why?" She waited through a long moment of milk glass designs. "Connie?"

"We . . . may get married."

"Married?" And she suddenly heard an old song, one of the heavy 78's they used to play on the phonograph in the basement. She wanted to do something, make some response, clap her hands, gush, something sisterly and affectionate. She felt an odd deflation, Connie's statement both startling and anticlimactic. "What about dad?" Shreds of the scratchy old record ran through her head: " . . . down in the cellar where it used to be bare, my Mr. Right's keeping his coffins there . . . my man's an undertaker, he's got a coffin just your size . . ."

"What about him?" Connie hunched her shoulders. "You know, I think it's about time somebody else thought about . . . " a hand waved in vague dismissal. "I'm sorry, I didn't mean . . . It's not anything we're rushing into." A smile without humor. "We're not kids. It's just something to . . . think about settling." Musing. "Oh, wouldn't tongue's wag?" She didn't motion toward the narrow hallway, toward the cough, but Sharon sensed an inner gesture in that direction. "We may have to start thinking about a nursing home or something." Hurriedly, "He's not getting any easier to take care of and lately he's been acting . . . Well, you know how it is, people get old."

A spasm of actual hatred, so fierce she blinked. Would the idea of abandoning dad have come up before this "Mr. Eustice" thing? She was aware of moving her own glass in neat squares and put her hands in her lap. This was turning into one of those interminable, organ-echoed, incomplete conversations from afternoon television. "I'd hate to see that." Lame. A bit stronger: "I don't think he'd be happy somewhere else, with strangers, shut up in a little room."

Connie ignored the smoldering cigarette in the ash tray, lit another one. Sharon stubbed the old one out. "I'm not talking about shoving him out to the poorhouse, you know. But he needs proper care, people who know how . . . "

"Oh, Connie, I know that." Her fingers fluttered, squeezed her sister's wrist, stroked the prominent knuckles. "It's just that . . . " There were no words to complete the sentence; she wasn't sure what she wanted to say. Something about the feeling of permanence here, his being here when she came, the rough comfort of that cough. Connie nodded, misinterpreting.

"Shar, I'm almost forty years old." But no despair in that—or lost in a neutral curiosity, the statement simply hung out.

An irrational urge to giggle, seeing Mr. Eustice in the bedroom, bony, naked below the waist, limp, approaching the bed in starched white shirt and shined shoes. In one corner of the room, the old white dresser and the little wicker chairs. She wanted to cry.

"I know he's a bother, but . . . "

"Shar, just for a little while I'd like . . . "

Why couldn't they finish sentences? "I thought you were pretty happy, Connie."

Joel's forehead seemed cooler. If it rained tomorrow, if they

couldn't go outside . . . She adjusted the cover, turning down the
damp edge. His small face was a wedge cutting down to a pointed
chin where Earl's was round. Hillary's face was like Earl's. But both
children looked like Earl. Something in the eyes, the way their eyebrows were already settling into the perpetual frown, even when
they laughed, grooving the skin above the nose. Earl was in the
center of the bed again, the thin cover a damp tangle around his
waist. His heavy breathing made the room hot, close. He made the
room—*her* room—small and foreign.

The yard was misty. She stood by the window, unconsciously
stroking herself. The rain had stopped for a while and the moon
shivered behind a murky film. Connie *had* let the gardening go; the
kudzu vine hulked near the roses, threatening them with its mass.
When she was small, during Lent . . . She pressed her forehead
against the window pane.

Mr. Eustice's house was a dark lump in the night. He was so old.
Fifty? Would Connie move across the yard to his house, or would he
come to live here, sit in her father's chair, follow his mower under
the pear tree and around the kudzu vine?

She took one of the cardboard tubes from her suitcase and fum-
bled with it in the darkness, then crawled onto the tilted mattress,
curling herself into a ball. Her back ached. She knew she wouldn't
be able to sleep and stared at the lighter dark of the window. Something, perhaps the coughing, a faint dry rustle, woke her. It had
started. She fell asleep again, the relief a brief and fragile thing.

At the Border

The old man drove carefully. It had rained during the afternoon as usual. The tires were worn to smooth rubber skins and here, near the border, where the shell holes from the skirmishes last spring had not been filled, the truck slewed in puddles of sticky water. The sky was clear now and the road would soon be dry until it rained tomorrow.

The sedan in front of the old man's truck speckled the windshield with wet clay spots. In the rear view mirror, framed in canvas, he could see the other truck and two other cars following. He could also see the inside of his truck. The terrorist was sitting very straight, bouncing up and down with his back rigid. The guards, one on each side and three on the wooden-slatted bench opposite, rode with the truck's motion, their bodies loosely adapting to the irregular tilt and lurch.

"It won't be long now," the lieutenant said.

The old man nodded, but didn't take his eyes off the road. He was a good driver, cautious, alert; he had learned it didn't prove anything to drive like a crazy man with only one hand on the wheel.

"It would have been better to shoot him," the lieutenant said, and, from the corner of his eye, the old man saw the limp backward movement of the lieutenant's hand. "One less to worry about."

"Maybe," the old man said. That was a safe thing to say, neutral, agreeable without being agreement. The lieutenant was young and thought shooting people was simple and final. The old man understood that. He felt the same way when he was young and a lieutenant. Now, after the see-saw of years, so many promotions and court-martials he didn't remember them all, he was reasonably content with his low rank and his truck. As a driver he didn't even have the weight of a weapon to burden him.

He eased to a stop behind the captain's car and set the brake. It was a good place for the business, here at the border; the other side chose well. There was a stretch of flat rocky ground on either side of the canted signpost and from the other side, unseen, they could watch the approach road. On the other side of the border the trees were close enough so they could disappear quickly as soon as it was over. And this section of the border was remote enough from the capital to discourage patrols. The leaders on the other side were clever people, obviously, and there was a good chance by the next dry season there would be someone new in the presidential palace and a different lieutenant declaring that shooting was simple.

The captain approached and the old man saluted carefully as he did everything else. The salute was proper—anyone on this side of the border could see that—and yet did not betray anything more than the gesture required of a low-ranking military man, did not suggest here was a man who fawned on his officers or eagerly suported the regime's policies—and anyone watching from the other side of the border could see that.

The captain, flanked by the men in suits, walked to the back of the truck and waited impatiently while the guards climbed out and stood at attention. One of them had been dozing—his eyes were blank, unfocused—and the captain flicked him with a glance, bringing him sullenly awake. The terrorist jumped down and held himself stiffly as though he, too, was at attention. His wrists were handcuffed behind him.

The terrorist needed a shave and his eyes were pushed in with fatigue. The old man noticed that the terrorist had only two bruises, a plum-colored swelling on the forehead and a red abrasion, crosshatched with tiny cuts, on his cheekbone. They couldn't have questioned him very vigorously unless they worked on his stomach and groin. But if that had happened he wouldn't be standing so straight.

"We ought to shoot him," the lieutenant said. He didn't say it loudly enough for the captain to hear, but one of the men in suits glared. "It's not worth it."

The old man—he wasn't really that old, barely fifty, but he felt old and was treated as an old man; perhaps it was the lines in his face or the way he spoke (or avoided speaking) or his posture—rested his hip and shoulder against the truck. Was it worth it? Probably not. Unless you were the terrorist or the tourist. Then you thought it was worth it.

They were here, the old man, the terrorist, the captain, the men in suits, the lieutenant, the others, to exchange the terrorist for a kidnapped tourist. It was the fourth—no, the fifth—time the old man had been on such a mission.

He wanted a cigarette. Pretty soon someone else—the captain or one of the men in suits—would light one and then he could safely light his.

Kidnapping the tourist, that was clever, the old man thought. Not new, but clever. Why the abduction of a single tourist should cause more fuss than blowing up a bus or throwing a bomb in a movie or ambushing a colonel's car the old man didn't know, but it did. When a tourist was kidnapped reporters bumped into each other, there was a frantic scooting of jeeps in the streets and the president came on the radio to denounce it as a terrible thing. The president appealed to world opinion to put a stop to such acts and men in suits with pomade on their hair looked very solemn and drove miles over bad roads to the border to add the impressive weight of the government to what was happening. Not three miles from here, four men—not friends exactly, but men the old man knew well, men he drank with, played cards with, ate pepper sausage with—were grenaded to little pieces and no one in a suit came. That didn't bother the old man. Someone in a suit with talcum on his closely shaved cheeks and an expensive gold watch on his wrist couldn't put all the little pieces together and make someone to drink and eat and play cards with, but it was strange all the same. The tourist wasn't even an important man. If he had been, there would be different men in suits, the heads of ministries with bodyguards, and at least a colonel would be in charge.

The terrorist was standing very straight, holding his head up so the muscles in his thin neck stretched taut. He was young—but then, most of them were. Standing very straight like that (his legs were going to cramp soon, the old man knew) he was trying to prove something. It was like driving like a crazy man with one hand on the wheel.

There, the captain had a cigarette and the lieutenant was quickly leaning forward to light it. Everyone relaxed a little and the old man leaned invisibly against the truck, softly scratched a match and enjoyed the smoke in his mouth.

The men in suits looked at their watches and pinched their mouths and that irritated the captain. He folded his arms tight across his chest, looked beyond the border at the empty space creeping into the trees, walked in a tight circle staring at the polished tips of his boots.

"Five minutes," the captain said.

"We have to wait—" one of the men in suits said.

"Five minutes!" The captain said it loudly, too loudly, as though he wanted someone on the other side of the border to hear. The terrorist stood very straight, disdainful of what was happening, trying to prove something to his audience or himself, trying to show he was taller, a bigger man, than the soldiers around him.

The old man hoped they would bring the tourist soon. In another hour it would be dark and it would turn cold. He didn't like to drive at night. It had nothing to do with mines—you could run over a mine at noon—but his eyes watered and he got a headache when he had to squint at the road at night. And if he got a flat tire he would have to get out in the cold and fix it himself while the lieutenant sat in the cab smoking cigarettes or, worse, stood beside him keeping his uniform clean and urging the old man to hurry as though the flat tire was the old man's fault and he enjoyed squatting in the cold.

He was glad they didn't bring the tourist's wife this time. Once they did that and it made everyone nervous. The old man wasn't superstitious, but he thought the flat tire that night had something to do with the wife being there.

It was odd, this kidnapping of tourists. Odd that each time it happened there was such a strong reaction, so much fuss raised.

The old man knew the pattern.

In the night three or four men in uniform come, tap on the tourist's door. They are just more men in uniform, no one nearby seems to notice. Who knows if they are terrorists in stolen uniforms or are really from the army? Maybe the tourist has been doing something foolish with the currency or has been taking pictures in an unauthorized place or has stolen something from one of the churches, one of the "treasures of the people." Or perhaps the tourist is a spy or a saboteur or knows someone who is a spy or has brought in subversive literature in his luggage. Or perhaps the government just wants to question him for one of the infinite reasons the government has for coming at night to knock on the door. It's better not to notice, not to say, not to know anything because if you don't mind your own business three or four men in uniform—maybe terrorists, maybe army—will come to the witness's door and on and on. These things happen. It's better to go about your business.

The old man knew how it went, could see it all as though he was watching one of the old, old movies for the twentieth time at the Grand Movie Palace. He had been an officer himself at times when these things happened.

So.

The knock, the protests, the husband in the car. The wife is angry, goes to the authorities. Why have they arrested her husband? She may be hastily dressed, but she is wearing cosmetics. They always take time for that.

Ah (so politely), the officer at the desk says. Most assuredly a check will be made and it is recommended the lady should go back to the hotel and rest but, no, she is angry, will not budge, demands implores demands. The officer (probably a captain) disappears, reappears. Regretfully, there is no record of Mr. So-and-so. Who knows what is happening? Perhaps the terrorists, the enemies of the state, have taken the husband. Perhaps the army has him and, for some secret official reason, does not wish to disclose it, will wait for a while before making the arrest formal. Of course (the captain says) an investigation will be made promptly because this is a serious matter. Of course it will be looked into at once. Just for the record, has Mr. So-and-so (regrettably, these questions are necessary) been involved in—ah—"political" activity? No, no, the question is absurd. Then could, perhaps, the wife be mistaken? Could—only a suggestion; the officer means no offense, will phrase it as nicely as he can—Mr. So-and-so perhaps simply have gone with friends to indulge in—ah—an evening of male conviviality? No no no no. Now she is angry, but a touch of uncertainty, of dread, colors the anger and she shouts to disguise it. Wasn't the captain listening to anything she said? How can she be mistaken about this? Didn't the captain pay attention? Her husband has been arrested, abducted, something . . .

Would she, then, be so good as to describe these men who came to her door in the night? Of course not. How can she? It was dark. She was half asleep. It happened so quickly. Besides, everyone in this country looks the same and—oh oh. The captain smiles so softly, his face is so bland. Yes that *is* a problem, isn't it. No, no, she didn't mean—she was flustered, worried . . . Now the fear is a cold snake slowly uncoiling in her stomach. Go back to the hotel, inquiries will be made, measures will be taken, forms will be filled out as required at some future unspecified time. Go back to the hotel go home go away.

The old man held the smoke in his mouth, let is escape deliciously through his nostrils.

Now the hotel room is not only hot and dusty (yes, just a little dusty. It is the wind. And it has lizards, no doubt about that. The old man knows this because there is not a room in the city that is not dusty, hot, inhabited by a harmless lizard or two at this time of year), but it is smaller. Definitely smaller. Through the night it shrinks in on her, grows hotter even though the night is cool, almost cold. She will be angry only now and then, uneasy not at all. She is through with that. Frightened. Yes, this she is, more and more. Everyone who passes the window, anyone passing in the hall, will move with strange purpose, will be an enemy. She thinks the night will never end, thinks it has never been this dark and this long before. She consoles herself with the thought that everything is worse at night.

It seems the night will never end. But it does. And in the daylight it is worse because everything around her *seems* so normal. People are having breakfast, there is laughter, the clink of spoons in cups, conversation. Isn't he cute? Don't forget the camera. Sunshine. In the afternoon, rain. Everything *seems* normal: beggars dust the heavy sweet smell of fruit heat dust laughter dust. This strange place covers the gap where the husband should be.

These things happen, the old man knew.

But then a note is delivered. Mr. So-and-so will be released in exchange for Comrade Such-and-such.

"Two minutes," the captain said loudly and the lieutenant's eyes touched the terrorist. The terrorist looked very haughty, like a movie star in a picture where the hero carries a sword and sometimes sings, trying to prove something. The terrorist probably thought he looked lean and dangerous. The old man thought he looked hungry. Unless the terrorist was one of the rare crazy ones, one of the few who fed himself on rage and simple solutions and wanted to be a martyr, he was frightened under the pose. The old man could have told him that was all right, there was nothing to be ashamed of, that all sensible men are afraid most of the time. But of course that wouldn't do any good.

"I won't wait much longer," the captain said, looking at his watch.

The old man yawned. The five minutes had passed and everyone, even the captain, knew it was a meaningless deadline. They would wait here through the night if necessary.

The guards relaxed. The men in suits whispered together, looked at the terrorist as though he were something inanimate, a piece of dubious fruit on a vendor's cart, whispered again. They were careful to separate themselves from the military men, to show they were important government people. The old man loosened his knees and let the truck support him. The government men were trying to show they were separate and important; the captain had drawn a small invisible circle of authority around himself; the lieutenant, too, made his own smaller circle, but at the same time he tried to edge into the captain's space, to share his superior's importance. And the terrorist was standing very straight, pretending he was twice as tall as the guards around him. The old man yawned again.

"There they are," one of the guards said and there was a sudden change of mood. Not tension but anticipation, something almost festive. A collective release. Now something would happen. Even the old man felt it. Now he wouldn't have to drive at night, might even be home in time to have some soup. His wife would keep it warm until midnight.

Across the border a group of men was moving out of the black shape of the trees. Whoever selected this place wasn't stupid, the old man thought again. The sun was dropping toward the trees and the captain and his men had to squint into it while he and the lieutenant and the others were in bright light and made good targets.

"Stay here," the captain said. He slapped his leg and began to march toward the border as though he was parading past the presidential box, his polished boots making firm little smacks on the bare ground.

The government men whispered busily and then started after the captain. "Stay here," one of them said to the lieutenant. It was the one who had glared when the lieutenant suggested shooting the terrorist.

The lieutenant watched the circles of authority moving away. He crossed his arms and looked important. "Stay here," he told the guards. He unsnapped the walnut-colored leather strap on his holster. "Watch him carefully." He hurried after the captain and the men in suits, trying hard not to appear to be hurrying.

The old man yawned again, took off his cap and scrubbed his hair. He examined his fingernails and wiped them on his tunic. He hoped it wouldn't take long. If they would just agree to exchange the terrorist and the tourist he would be home long before midnight. But if the terrorists made speeches the government men would probably want to make speeches, too.

He crunched his hat on his head, tugging the visor low so it shielded his eyes, and sighed. The terrorists were close to the border marker and four of them were carrying something. That meant trouble and trouble meant delay. But perhaps the tourist was only sick, his legs weak from the belly trouble tourists often had. That would be good. The exchange would be quick.

Beyond the border the terrorists had moved away from the black bulk of the trees and were crossing the slab of light. Their shadows were much larger than they were, immensely long and narrow, probing the feet of the captain and the men in suits, sliding over the ground to stab at the lieutenant as he hurried to catch up.

The terrorists tenderly placed their burden on the ground, letting it rest on the invisible line that was the border, half of the still shape on either side. The old man watched the captain and the men in suits stare at it. One of the civilians squatted, adjusting his trousers to preserve the crease. He must have said something to the captain because the captain bent his head, slapped his leg twice, then straightened and stood with his hands on his hips. He made an impressive silhouette with the sharp angles of his elbows and the long clean lines of his legs casting a shadow back toward the men by the truck.

The old man could see that the terrorists all had machine guns suspended from the straps around their shoulders and resting on their hip bones. Their range wasn't great and it was impossible to aim them accurately, but, for some reason, machine guns were very popular with terrorists. Probably, the old man thought, because they make a lot of noise and you didn't have to be a marksman to use one. The machine gun was a simple weapon.

The lieutenant lifted an arm and shouted for four men to come to the border. The captain turned his head and he must have said something because the lieutenant dropped his arm and started back toward the truck. When he came close the old man could see his face was flushed. He felt disgraced because he had been sent back, away from the circles of authority.

The lieutenant told three of the men to take the terrorist—"Shoot him if he makes the slightest false move!"—to the captain. He pointed to the old man. "You." He poked his finger at three others. "You, you—and you there. Come with me. The rest of you be ready for anything."

The terrorist marched with his back stiff, kept his head held high. The guard on his right, a young man, almost a boy, awkwardly lengthened his strides to keep pace and fingered his rifle.

The men in suits wore the same expression, irritated and embarrassed. They were already framing their explanations to their superiors. The captain looked angry. The old man saw the tourist was dead, had been dead for at least a day. He was surprised at how old the tourist was. The rumpled dusty hair was as bluish-gray as the face. There was a sprinkle of grayish beard on the sagging cheeks.

"It was an accident," one of the terrorists said. The old man looked at him. The terrorists were standing in a loose semi-circle. The man who said it was an accident was a little older than the others, but not much older.

"An accident," the captain said. He did not look so angry now. His face was calm, but there were white indentations at the corners of his mouth.

The older terrorist shrugged. "An accident," he said again. "Unfortunate but . . ." his shrug was a weary lift of his shoulders, "these things happen." He did not sound as though he believed it was unfortunate, did not sound as if he cared much one way or the other. The old man noticed the terrorist with his hands handcuffed behind him wore a very slight smile.

The captain pinched his nose with his fingers. "Unfortunate, yes." He looked at the prisoner for a long time, then he and the older terrorist across the border studied each other. No one looked at the dead tourist. "These things happen," the captain said. "Lieutenant, your pistol."

Two men in suits stepped forward together, began to protest, saying identical things about "authority" and "instructions." the captain told them to be quiet. He said it softly and they closed their mouths and stepped back, creating an isolating space around themselves.

The lieutenant handed his pistol to the captain and saluted smartly, but the captain ignored the salute. He massaged the bridge of his nose with the pistol. He was looking at the prisoner, but seemed to be looking through and beyond him. The old man saw that the lieutenant's pistol was well cared for. Light from the sun beyond the border ran in a quick liquid streak along the oiled barrel. The captain shifted his eyes to the older terrorist.

"An equal exchange." He said it quietly, politely. The terrorists beyond the border stiffened, shifted their machine guns. The older man made a slight gesture with his hand.

The terrorist with his hands cuffed behind him blinked. The captain slowly, gently, placed the barrel of the pistol between the young man's eyes and the young man's eyes involuntarily crossed. He shut his eyes and swallowed hard, then opened his eyes to stare at the captain.

The old man saw the captain's hand was clean, small-boned, almost feminine. He saw the thumbnail was manicured as the thumb rolled the hammer back. The double click was sharp and loud.

For what seemed a long time the only sound was the sun moving down toward the trees.

Suddenly the young man began to weep silently. He looked down the length of the pistol past the delicate thumb into the captain's eyes and his shoulders slumped. "Please," he said. And then, louder, "please."

The captain eased the hammer forward. He handed the pistol to the lieutenant who did not return it to its holster but held it at his side.

"Pick him up," the captain said. The old man and three of the guards picked up the tourist, juggling him for an instant until his weight was distributed. The old man grunted. The tourist was heavier than he looked. "Go ahead," the captain said. He gave the young man a push, not hard, and the man with his hands cuffed behind his back and the dust on his face streaked with tears stumbled across the border.

The terrorists turned and moved away. The young man with the bound hands seemed still to be a prisoner in the circle of young men with machine guns.

Led by the captain and the lieutenant and the men in suits, the old man and the guards walked back toward the truck. The short burst of machine gun fire, seven or eight shots so close together they made a single ragged ripping sound, startled them so they ducked instinctively and almost dropped the tourist. Everyone but the old man and the captain looked back at the black mass of trees swallowing the sun, leaving only a pomegranate-colored slice pasted on the sky. The old man took advantage of the pause to change his hold on the tourist. He took a deep breath and eased the strain on his back. The lieutenant was grinning.

The men in suits looked at each other, bewildered. "He disgraced

himself, crying like that," the lieutenant said. He sounded happy.
The old man was breathing heavily when they reached the truck.
"All right, put him in the back," the lieutenant said.
"No," the captain said.
They stood looking at the captain. He was pinching his nostrils
again, studying the tourist suspended between them with the expres-
sion he wore just before he placed the gun on the young man's nose;
he seemed to be looking through the tourist at some point far away.
Then he turned and looked back at the border.

"Hold him up." The captain stood beside the old man and lifted
the blanket with thumb and forefinger, peeled it back off the stiff
legs, worked it off the body. The old man noticed the captain's
fingers did not tremble at all as he gently pried the plastic bomb
from the frozen cavity of the tourist's armpit and eased the contact
detonator out. "They put him down very carefully for a dead man,"
the captain said. His voice was even, almost bored, but the old man
saw a tiny beading of sweat on his lip.

The lieutenant's eyes were wide. "Bastards," he said. The men in
suits looked at each other with mouths identical holes.

Even though there was no danger now the old man and the guards
put the tourist in the truck as though he were fragile and the guards
kept their feet tucked well under the wooden-slatted benches away
from the body.

In the cab the lieutenant stared through the windshield. He
repeated "bastards" in a low voice. The captain put his hand on the
old man's door with his fingers curled over the rolled-down window.

"Drive carefully, eh," he said. He was smiling.

The old man nodded and disengaged the brake. He tried to think
of his wife's soup. It would be a long drive. He had a headache as
though he had been squinting at the road at night.

A Simple Dying

She said: "My father committed suicide."

"Oh?"

"With a shotgun. Twelve gauge." Terse, factual.

"Ernest Hemingway, the writer, did that." It was one of his own facts, carried unedited and unexamined from high school like the fact of Washington's wooden teeth. "I don't remember if it was a twelve gauge."

"My father used a twelve gauge." As if this were the standard by which to judge. "He didn't leave a note. Most suicides leave a note. Know why?"

"No," he said, wondering why Martha bothered with this. There was something in her voice, a time-colored tone. Either she was telling it again, just this way, or she had rehearsed it. He wondered if she was talking to him or her mother or herself.

"Because they don't think they're really going to die. Maybe they think they really can't go on, but they don't think it's really going to end, either. It's—well, it's like they feel they're only going away a little bit, just changing around, moving—oh, aside to—well, to someplace else where they can watch what's happening and when people realize how bad they've been treated they can come back some way . . ."

Her mother snorted, a croak of wet disgust, and hitched her chair around so she was facing away from them, her nose pointing out over the porch railing toward the river. The quiet that came with the end of each day during the late summer had settled in. The trees

were heavy and still along the banks, thick merging bouquets of
bronze and scarlet; the river a smooth yellowish-grey. Above the
trees, a very pale green sky marbled with lavender and peach.
    Martha was talking in the same flat saying-it-again voice. "It's
kind of sad when you think on it. They're just scared little people,
trying to get people to pay attention. Or they think they'll teach
someone a lesson so they leave notes that don't sound like them talking at all and they think they'll just be off someplace, kind of invisible, watching people read the notes and fussing about and feeling
sorry for how bad it was . . ."
    "The potatoes were sour," her mother said. She was especially
peckish. Probably the heat, he thought. Or maybe she didn't want
to be reminded of what happened to her husband.
    "They weren't sour. They weren't anywhere near sour. Did you
think they were sour?"
    He couldn't remember the potatoes. "No, I don't think so."
    "They were as good as any potatoes, weren't they?"
    "They were fine." In gravy? Boiled? Sulking under a congealing
skin of milk-sodden cheese? Come to think of it, every time he came
to dinner there were potatoes. After they were married would she go
on presenting him with potatoes at every meal? He didn't even par-
ticularly like potatoes, but, until now, it wasn't important enough to
mention. Suddenly it was another of the unconsidered little threats
the future held. Now that her mother had said "sour" in that
poisonously nasal way, there was a slight burning in the back of his
mouth, a peculiar salty taste. Come to think of it, where was her
mother going to be while he was eating potatoes? Right there at the
table with him?
    The old lady was smiling. How did he know that? Her back was
turned, but he could *feel* her smile, see it in the hard curve of her
shoulders.
    "Your father was a fine-looking man." What else was there to
say? And it was true with a bland, an unexceptional truth. On the
ugly, crate-sized radio—he didn't know if it worked; it was never
played—Martha's father smiled out from a tan-cardboard frame.
Time had warped the frame into a slight vee so her father leaned forward in a permanent slouch. He had never thought much about the

man before, he was just Martha's father. He couldn't match the youngish man with her mother at all. The picture was simply a part of the room like the faded fabric of the bell-pull—that didn't work, either; he'd tugged it once just to see if anything happened—the limp oyster-tinted curtains, the plush on the cumbersome chairs aged from maroon to dark chocolate. The chairs themselves were uninviting, complacently fat and stolid as old ladies at a wake. The photograph had that quality of photographs of dead and unknown people, an impression of perpetual vacuity, insisting this is the way they were, not smiling for the camera, but smiling always.

He wasn't imaginative, but he shivered, seeing the man curled over, smiling into the shotgun's frozen "o."

"He *was* a fine man," Martha said as though to forestall her mother's denial.

"He was a *fine* man," her mother echoed. He believed she was smiling her pinched-lip smile that dug deep grooves like chisel strokes in her cheeks.

"He *was!*"

"Well, I *said* he was, didn't I?"

It was a mistake to come tonight; he knew that when he arrived to a brittle silence stretched like iced cords through the kitchen. When he bent to kiss her cheek he was aware of her eyes looking past him at her mother and her mother's quick, vicious slices with the knife at the sink.

"I'm sure he was," he said, wanting it to end. But as with the "sour" taste that, once mentioned, could not be erased, so it was with the image of the smiling man and the shotgun's barrel. At what instant did the smile vanish?

When he shifted, the swing's chains squealed. After dinner they always came out here and she sat on the railing while her mother planted herself in the fan-backed rocker. He would sit in the swing. It became a habit. At first he tried to change places, to get Martha to sit beside him, and was told, sharply, no, you sit there. Sit yourself down, now. He sat very still so the chains would not squeak against the rusted hooks impaling the wainscoted ceiling, but the slightest motion brought a protesting screech, no matter how carefully he held himself. By the time her mother announced she was going in

("Don't you stay out here too long, Martha, you'll take a chill"), his thighs would ache from keeping himself in one position.

Martha leaned back against the post carved in bulbous curves and ridges like bracelets, her weight on her left hip. Her leg swung in small precise arcs. He watched her skirt pull taut against thigh, a tiny race of pale light on her bare calf as her leg moved, and his throat tightened.

"It's a warm evening," he said. When her leg moved forward the skirt formed bottomless shadowy folds at her belly. She was looking past her mother at the flat stillness of the river, a dull plum-colored sheet now in the twilight. The trees were an indistinct smudge.

He didn't know Martha's mother's name, had never heard it mentioned. She had been introduced as "my mother" and he called her Mrs. Dow or a school-boy-polite "ma'am." When darkness eased over the porch and one of them spoke, he had to identify the voice by location because they sounded so much alike. Not that Martha sounded old—or that her mother's voice was young. There was a shifting quality in both voices, sliding variations around a neutral, ageless middle-tone. Sometimes, when her mother spoke softly, he thought it was Martha and, occasionally, when she was being snappish, Martha's voice was her mother's.

With the coming of night the crackling silence from the kitchen reappeared on the porch.

No one asked such questions, but, if someone had asked, he would have said her eyes were brown because he was uncomfortable with words that weren't simple and common. But, in his room, alone, he sometimes told himself her eyes were smoky quartz, the same color as the paperweight on his mother's dresser. Smoky quartz had a secret exotic sound and he tried to find other things that might be described, to himself, in those hard sheened and, at the same time, fragile words. Once, sitting on the porch, he said, "The river looks like smoky quartz," and he was a little surprised to find it did. A little. But Martha looked at him strangely and her mother's laugh was a sarcastic rip so that he was embarrassed and never again tried to describe anything in what he thought of as poetic words.

A solitary car passed on the river road, headlights a shuttered glow behind the trees.

He had told Martha he loved her, but had never gone beyond that, not even to himself. It was a statement and he had never said, "I love you because . . ." And Martha had never asked. Once, breathless after a long desperate kiss under the trees by the river, he asked, "Do you love me?" and he took her wordless, masculine hug for an answer. Even his proposal—not a request but another statement: "I'd like to marry you"—brought no definite response. She had squeezed him to her while he ran his palms up the thick resilient pads of flesh flanking her spine and then down over the rubbery curves of her buttocks—not spongy rubbery but firm as tractor tires—and her fingers kneaded his neck and shoulders with a painful insistence he took for passionate assent. After that he assumed they were engaged.

That night, back in his room, he had been disappointed because he wanted something more, a mutual declaration of "something" in words as tantalizing as smoky quartz. He tried to find comfort in the fading memory of her fingers on his nape.

"I'll get you a beer," Martha said. He knew it was Martha because the voice came from the porch railing—and because her mother would never volunteer. He touched her hand when she passed and let his fingers brush her leg. The swing-chains shrieked and her mother said, "I want some lemonade."

The screen door squeaked. The next time he came he'd bring some oil and take care of that. And the damned swing-chains, too. Sitting alone with her mother, even for a few minutes, made him uncomfortable. He couldn't think of anything to say and she didn't help. In fact, she seemed to be quiet on purpose, making short silences swell threateningly like balloons.

"It sure is warm," he said.

"Always is, this time of year. Be queer if it wasn't." Her voice was very like Martha's. She didn't have to say that and she didn't have to say it that way, as though he was too stupid to know it was always hot this time of year. He laughed because he didn't know what else to do and felt stupid because the laugh sounded forced and childish. A slight breeze, a movement of the warm air, rubbed the leaves on the vine limply clinging to the string trellis and he smelled the river.

He wanted to get up and go in with Martha, press her against the refrigerator, but he didn't want to make the chains screech. "I'm sorry about your husband," he said, hoping he sounded sympathetic. He saw the man in the picture, bent in a half-bow, smiling into the shotgun. Where did he do it? In the ugly room with its heavy, heat-trapping drapes? In the kitchen, with the butt wedged against a table leg, shifting around so the path of the pellets wouldn't shatter the row of glasses? Maybe right out here, right here sitting on the porch with the smell of the river crawling across the balding lawn?

"Things happen," her mother said and he felt her shrug. It was an odd answer.

Why hadn't George ever mentioned it, Mr. Dow shooting himself? You'd think, much as George talked, he'd mention something like that. Come to think of it, George talked all the time—in the three months he'd been at the garage there probably weren't ten minutes all of a piece when George wasn't talking about *some*thing—but he didn't really talk about any one thing, just jabbered away. Well, he did say she—Mrs. Dow—had money, but how she came to have it or how much it was, he never did mention. Of course he hadn't told George—or anybody else, since he didn't talk to people much—about Martha being his fiancé. It just wasn't a thing you could come right out and say, for one thing. And he couldn't afford a ring yet and to be properly engaged there should be a ring. He had almost enough saved for the one in Bollit's window, a really nice one on a plump bed of white satin in a blue velvety-looking box, but that was going to be a problem, too. He couldn't just march Martha in there and have her see how much it cost, that wouldn't be right. You were supposed to give her the ring in a proper place. But if he bought it and it didn't fit, what could he do? If he had to exchange it and they didn't have another one the same price . . . well, there was no hurry on it, but he'd have to work out something.

"Well, it's a real shame, what he did, I mean." He wished Martha hadn't said anything about it, at least not with all that other stuff about not leaving a note or anything, making it something special.

"You're from up near Tuscoma?"

"Yes, ma'am."

"Ahhhh," as though that explained something.

"How old are you?"

"Me?"

She didn't repeat the question and he flushed. It was a habit, asking questions like that when he was startled or needed time to think. She hitched her chair around so she was facing him. He could barely make out the vague greyish blur of her face.

"I'm twenty-four."

"Martha's going on thirty."

He didn't know that. "Yes, ma'am." What could he say to that? "She's a really fine woman—girl—though." A stupid thing to say.

"He did leave a note. Start of one anyway." A statement as uninflectioned as the man on the radio telling about the stock market.

He took a deep breath. "Maybe I better go help Martha."

"She doesn't need any help."

"No, ma'am." He cringed; the chains made a sound like a saw ripping tin.

"You can ask her. She won't tell you about it, but you can ask her. Oh, he left a note." Her voice was no longer neutral. "Make you sick to your stomach to read it, full of whiney nonsense . . ." Had there really been a note or was the old lady just making it up, being vicious for some reason he couldn't figure out and didn't want to? What did he care anyway? He didn't tell Martha about his father; he didn't even think much about his father himself. Every day his father went to work and one day he came home with the cold sweats and the next day, no matter what was said to him, he dragged himself back to the mill and two days later he was dead. And that was that. Wasn't that like killing himself? But he didn't go around telling people about it. He didn't want to hear any more about Martha's father or notes, but, with the old lady, there was suddenly nothing else to talk about. It was blessed hard to change the subject from suicide notes. What was taking Martha so long? He heard the faint gurgling splash from the chain-pull flush.

"It must have been hard for you," he said.

"It made a mess." *That* wasn't what he meant at all. "Martha threw the note away."

"Just threw it away?"

"Threw it away, burned it, how do I know? Got rid of it." Her voice wasn't like Martha's now; it wasn't even like her own. It came out of the darkness in hard shiny pieces, sharp as glass splinters. "Couldn't *bear* to have that self-pitying scrap of drivel to prove to everybody what he was."

"Well, I'm sorry, I truly am." That was safe enough to say. He could be sorry for Mr. Dow or Martha or even the old woman or all of them at once. What he was really sorry for was that any of this came up to pester him. He had a fleeting vision of Martha slowly tearing up a piece of paper and flushing the scraps away.

"That was Dow's favorite word. Sorry. No end to his 'sorrying.' Always sorry about something. Sorry he couldn't bring himself to finish the note, sorry he was too tired to finish patching the roof, sorry he didn't have the gumption to finish . . ." She made a curious, strangely disgusted sound. "Dow just never had it in him to finish anything."

He was standing in the swing-chains' echo when Martha bumped the door with her hip and balanced the lacquered tray on the railing.

"I'm sorry you went and did that. I didn't realize how late it was getting to be. I've got to be at the garage early to get Mr. Keenan's Packard ready . . ." he was talking too fast. (Had he imagined the old lady's snort at his "sorry"?) "He's going to Troy first thing in the morning and George, you know how George is, he promised we'd have it ready to go by eight . . ."

"I'm sorry you have to go and rush off," Martha said. She didn't sound sorry. She didn't sound much of anything.

At the gate he turned and waved, but couldn't see if she waved back. He didn't know why he lied. The Packard was tuned up so it purred, had been since five o'clock.

He had the devil of a time going to sleep and, just as he felt himself slipping away, he remembered what she, the old lady, said about Mr. Dow not finishing anything. Suddenly, wide awake, he saw the old woman fingering the shotgun and making those queer, strangely disgusted grunts.

The night was warm and smelled of dust. He walked for better than an hour before a trucker dead-heading to Preston picked him up and, by dawn, he was in Tuscoma.

Vandals

Each time, there were changes: a few more little shops with plywood instead of plate glass; an empty apartment with only empty sockets for windows; a movie house with blank marquee. This year an entire block had been razed. Acme Container, last year a three-story shell of blackened brick, was a rubbled pit, sprinkled with weeds. He shook his head. The changes were never improvements.

As he drove through the gate he turned off the radio, a concession to place. The gravel crunching under rubber seemed unnecessarily loud. As usual, he did not go directly to the graves but followed the twisting limestone track past the dusty cones of twin firs he used as a landmark (thinking, again, with pleasurable guilt, that either one would make a dandy Christmas tree). The Old Man loved Christmas. One of those family clichés, glued to a name as identification, something to evoke a personality: "Ed gets a bigger kick out of Christmas than the kids." Always said with a mock reproof and a gentle smile and the Old Man would say when he was a kid, no matter how bad things were, there was always something special about Christmas.

He shook his head again. Mixed with the gentle smile and his memories of the Old Man, he heard her later. Her voice would mush the last few words: "Ed got a bigger kick out of Christmas than the kids did. Remember?" They would all nod, say that was right, contribute some little verification. But it wasn't true. Through the last grey days of December it was a shared and escalating delight, something equally strong in them and the Old Man. After supper the Old

Man would announce, as if he'd just thought of it, "Well, I've got a few things to do." One of them (they had learned this was part of it) would ask what things and, looking very stern, he would say, "Just some things. Never mind what." And he would stomp down to the basement workshop where, behind the forbidden door, they would hear the sander's whine, the whispered rasp of the scroll saw, his tuneless whistle. On Christmas morning there would be four clumsily wrapped packages in identical 'special' paper topped with huge store-bought bows. The Old Man would sit with his slippered feet on the hassock, trying to look as if he was bored and under the wispy mustache the grin would threaten, retreat, threaten again, stronger. They always unwrapped those packages last. When they were older their surprised exclamations were a little forced because the Old Man really wasn't handy and the book-ends were always a bit lopsided, the dowels on the tie-racks never quite the same length, the hinges on Janet's cigar-box jewelry case improperly aligned so the lid didn't close completely but lifted one corner in a sneer—

When he crunched past the fir trees the inevitable mood of dissatisfaction sifted into the car, rode beside him. He followed the chalky line through the empty space—he still thought of it as the empty space, as it had been ten years ago when the section was only grassy knolls; now it was filling up and was no different from any other section—to the low humped bridge over the narrow stream. The stream seeped out of the clay hills to the north, just beyond the mills, filtered into the cemetery through a screen of sagging fence, widened into a miniature lake a few yards in front of the bridge, and then wandered out through another section of rusting fence to form a cat-tail spiked groove beside the B & O grade.

He paused on the bridge, motor idling, to look for the swans, but he couldn't see them. Crumbled blossoms of wax paper and disintegrating cans clustered along the banks. After the Old Man died he brought his mother out, once every two weeks during the few years she outlived the Old Man, and she always brought a small brown paper sack of crumbs for the swans, a paper sack and a paper-mache pot of whatever flowers were in season. After she put the flower pot beside the headstone she would kneel on the grass, pulling out a stray weed the groundskeepers had missed (but there weren't many;

they had really done a good job then of keeping the place neat, the weeds pulled, the grass trimmed and watered, the litter picked up). Then she would stand and look around vaguely for someplace to put the weeds. She would always sigh and drop them behind the headstone and dust her hands. By this time he was usually restless.

The first few times they came he knelt beside her and tried to imagine the Old Man lying in the maroon metal casket with its bronze handles, looking as he did during the last weeks, eyelids grainy and transparent as a moth's wing, the mustache a smudge of dirty lint in the center and yellowed at the corners. He would try to picture the Old Man sitting in the kitchen or with his feet on the hassock, but he kept seeing him lying under the ground, not really dead and not looking as he had in the funeral home with his cheeks artificially pink and his hair combed in an unnatural shingle, but as he had been toward the end in the bedroom at home, chest arched, caught in mid-breath, trying to pull air into his rotting lungs, the skin of his temples oily with the veins dark blue and ropey in the hollows, a glassy greenish bubble ballooning at one nostril.

He would kneel beside her, but he didn't know what to do. He wanted to say some kind of prayer, but the words that formed weren't really a prayer at all, were just a jumbled plea directed at no one in particular for the Old Man not to die and they sounded insincere in his head. After the first few times he didn't kneel and, after a month, he couldn't believe there was anything under the flattening mound so he stood with his hands in his pockets and waited until she finished.

After she dusted her hands she would take the old pot (the limp and bloomless stalks joined the weeds behind the headstone) back to the car and they would drive to the little bridge while she said, after a long silence, "I miss him, Frank," and he would nod, not knowing what to say to that, not wanting to answer with something that would start her off, wishing he could turn on the radio without seeming callous.

The swans, twin s-curves very white against the olive water and jade grass, moved in languid curls as she emptied the bag. She would say, "Your father always loved birds." Then, for some reason, she would say, "He never took much to dogs. Or cats, either— " a puzzled expression as she said this, a note of regret, and then, as though meeting some unspoken criticism, " —maybe because he was so poor when he was young, they couldn't afford a dog. But he loved birds, he really did." And *then,* inevitably, " . . . except pigeons, of course."

Then she would tell him the story of how, when she and Ed were first married and living in a little railroad flat on West 63rd, they had a parrot named Euell (with a wan smile: "Ed named him that. And, you know, it just seemed to fit him.") that Ed bought from a pet shop near the plant and someone who knew about birds said the parrot was at least seventy and Ed had cried like a baby—just like a baby, Frank—the morning they found it dead in its cage. It had drunk all its water during the night—every single drop, Frank. Ed wouldn't throw it in the trash, but took it three blocks away to a vacant lot and buried it."

It was a ritual: the visit to the grave, the flowers, the indecision with the weeds, feeding the swans, the comment on the Old Man's love of birds and, finally, the Euell story.

Once, impatient, he had asked, "If the Old Man loved birds so much, why the hell didn't he like pigeons—?"

Her eyes were wide and watery, a rind of pale red around the iris. "Oh, Frank— "

His voice was loud and the swans, alarmed, fled on overlapping fans of ripples. "I mean, a pigeon is a bird, too, for chrissake! Either he liked birds or he didn't!" Because he couldn't say, "Ma, you tell that same stupid story every time we come here!" and because it was more than that anyway, his anger grew.

She shook her head, wept with soggy grief, moved her hands in vague circles. He put his arm around her and mumbled apologies and excuses, blamed his sinuses, and was startled and frightened at how small she was, her arms both soft and thin under the imitation lamb coat, her fists and forehead pressed against his breastbone. He called her during the week and apologized again and she said it was all right, but she sounded dubious. He argued with his wife. Lena said it was morbid to go to the cemetery every two weeks and, because he thought it was, too, he argued viciously, attacking her habits. It was the first of their really bitter fights; not the first argument, but different in an ugly way, making reconciliation hard.

Two weeks later he brought her, with her paper sack and flower pot, back to the grave, prepared to listen, to encourage her pointless memories—but it was wasted preparation; she went through the ritual without prompting, right up to and through Euell, as though nothing had been said before. He worried about her mind then.

That night he called the others, but they didn't seem concerned. They said she was just getting old and you had to expect some changes. Janet said maybe they ought to start thinking about a home. Louie said Frank should try to get her mind on other things, get her out to meet new people.

He made excuses, invented reasons not to take her to the cemetery twice a month, thinking this might lessen her pain (and his own fear), but he found out she was taking a cab so he went back to driving her. Lena carefully figured out just how much gas he wasted doing this, presented an impressive list of figures with the total in red, and he said if Sandy could be driven way out to Brentwood every Saturday for a goddamn ballet lesson, he could afford to take his mother to visit his father's grave. Lena slammed cabinet doors and said if he couldn't see the difference between ballet lessons for a growing and talented child and squatting over a grave, if he couldn't see how *sick* the whole thing was, she could tell him, and he said ballet lessons for a six-year-old with two left feet at ten bucks a crack wasn't very bright, either, and he had to put his arm around her when she cried and he apologized, but it stayed between them.

He crossed the low bridge, turned the car around and came back to the twin firs, parked, walked up the small hill crowned with the statue of a Union soldier with a stone angel crouched at his feet. The soldier posed with head bowed and musket trailed on a marble octagon. In the early morning sunlight the chiseled FERGUSON was packed with shadows. There were bird droppings on the stone forage cap and he said, "pigeons," with disgust. He smiled when he said it. The statue, shaped from a softer stone than the base, was weather-streaked, watery yellow-green smears on grey stone. It reminded him of the statue in the Oscar Wilde story he had to listen to

Sandy read in a sing-song voice. Or the picture of Constantine's head on the postcard someone in the office sent from Italy.

He walked slowly up the hill. He would tell Lena that, about the Union soldier and Constantine's head. Not Wilde, that sounded childish. He would try to make her feel the wordless sadness of that moment, his solitary approach, the sunlight moving on the grass and the discolored soldier kind of melting away on his pedestal in the bright April morning. He patted the soldier's pitted toe as he passed and started down the gentle slope. He hoped he could find the postcard.

He stopped, bewildered.

Later, when he tried to describe it, he said his first reaction was outrage and, by then, he believed it. But his first reaction was bewilderment.

At first he thought he'd made a mistake, had come to the wrong place. He looked back at the soldier, then to the flat area at the base of the hill. It looked as though a monstrous wind had swept through. He took a few tentative steps, stopped, then ran the rest of the way (noting, with an odd detachment, that the grass was too long; the groundskeepers were not as conscientious as they used to be).

Some of the headstones were grotesquely tilted and, somewhere in the back of his mind, the impression he had seen something like that before. Others (older ones of light, cheap stone like sandstone with the dates and names almost erased by time and rain, the cherubs and flowers and scrollwork rubbed by weather until they were only meaningless bumps) were scattered, broken in jagged pieces. Five or six small ones, no larger than cinder blocks, were heaped under a willow. Where the stones had been ripped out there were ugly puckered holes in the earth. For some reason he remembered the immense hole in his jaw when he had a wisdom tooth extracted; he would touch the rim of the hole with his tongue, amazed at how wide and deep it seemed. Janet said it made her sick to see him poking his tongue around like that at the table and the Old Man had worried the middle of his grin, wire and slick pink imitation gum, out of his mouth and said when he had his teeth knocked clean out by a ninety-pound casting, why back in those days they didn't fuss with novacaine, you finished your shift, and his mother said, "Oh, Ed, not at the *dinner* table— !" as if there was a proper place to pluck your teeth out with saffron-tipped fingers . . .) This scene would come back to him later, again and again.

His parents' stone, the liver-colored marble once smooth as glass, was savaged. There must have been a flaw in the stone, some weak spot in the grain, and the sledge-hammer (nothing else could do that) had split it roughly down the middle. His mother's side was bent back, defaced, surrounded by small chips. Glancing blows of the hammer put queer indented commas in her name: MARY'ANN 'WARREN. A solid blow, leaving a mark like a heel print, obliterated the date of her birth. The Old Man's side was destroyed. One piece read EDWAR ; the others were too small to make out the letters.

He started to pick up the pieces, to arrange them in order on the ground. He stopped and turned in half-circles, hands raised helplessly. He could hear faint traffic sounds. He ran back to the car.

Near the gate, under a wall-less canvas tent, two men were sitting on a rolled tarpaulin, smoking. A yellow pick-up truck was parked in the shade of a few ancient pines. He stumbled from the car, yelling something (he could never remember, later, what he said and skipped over that part) and the two men watched his stumbling approach. They listened to him quietly. The younger man, with NICK stitched in pale blue thread over the pocket of his denim jacket, pinched out his cigarette, dropped the butt in the deep square hole, flicked dirt in on it with the side of his boot. The older man looked very sad or very bored. They followed his car in the pick-up truck and then he led them on foot over the hill past the soldier.

The young man lit another cigarette while his partner walked among the ruins, here and there touching a shard of stone with a clay-smeared toe.

"Looks like they dropped a fuckin bomb, don't it," the young man said conversationally. Frank thought he heard admiration in the voice. The older man said "kids" in tones of deep apathy or despair. He sent Nick back to the truck, told him to go over to maintenance and call the police and the super. The young man dropped his cigarette on the slight mound of a grave and Frank started to say something. The young man looked at him, then at the old man. The old man told him to hurry it up. Frank watched him walk away, hands wedged in hip pockets. The young man's hair was very long and looked greasy, spreading over his collar. Frank picked up the cigarette butt and put it in his pocket.

The old man asked Frank if he had people here. He didn't sound interested. He massaged the small of his back as if it ached. Frank pointed to the devastated headstone and the man said it was a shame, a real shame. He asked Frank if he was Jewish. Frank said of course not. He said it too loudly and the old man looked at him, then nodded.

Frank wanted to say something, to do something. He wanted the old man to tell him what was going to happen, but the old man wandered through the wreckage, touching pieces of stone with his toe. He whistled tunelessly through his teeth. The Old Man had whistled like that, an irritating hiss, when he was doing something around the house. With the pieces of the toaster spread out on the kitchen table mixed in with screw drivers and pliers and a coffee cup and a cigarette smouldering in the ash-tray shaped like a fish he would pick up various little gears and springs and would study them through half-closed eyes, all the while whistling unconsciously. Lamps, radios, clocks—he took them all apart on the kitchen table, whistled over them, carefully set the screws and bolts and springs aside in neat rows so he wouldn't lose them. He never really fixed anything. The dismembered remains would disappear into the basement workshop where they wound up in an immense cardboard box. After he died, Lou, Frank and Ernie went down to divide his tools and they shook their heads over twenty-year-old memories in pitted bronze, chipped porcelain, bent chrome. Ernie said, "Remember that?", holding up a handless clock with two battered brass bells on the case. They sat on dusty stacks of *Popular Mechanix* and *Handyman* in the basement, talking about the Old Man, and felt very sad and very close.

The sun was higher now and Frank took off his coat. His shirt was damp and sticky. He stood for a long time looking at the shattered headstone and he wanted to weep, felt an obligation to weep, tried, but couldn't.

The police came, almost resignedly, sirens silent, and the officer with the clipboard was sympathetic, but not, Frank thought, sincerely sympathetic. He talked to Frank as if he had rehearsed the phrases. His partner went over to the old man and Frank tried to hear what they said. The officer with the clipboard took Frank's name, address and asked his age.

"Forty-two," he answered automatically and was suddenly choked with anger. "What the hell difference does that make?" I mean, goddamnit, what the hell difference does *that* make— !?"

The visor almost touched the officer's nose and the sun slid on it like pale gold oil. Frank couldn't see his eyes, only a band of blind light. He told Frank to take it easy, that he knew how Frank felt, that it was routine. Frank answered the list of questions carefully; their very blandness, the officer's matter-of-fact tone, made Frank feel guilty, as though he was responsible. It was silly, but he couldn't help it. He had to sign a form and, while he was doing that, a reporter and a cameraman arrived. They drove around the soldier's knoll and parked on the grass beside the yellow pick-up. The reporter asked Frank questions that he answered without thinking while the cameraman walked around snapping pictures. Frank's hand shook and he jumped whenever the flashbulb threw its silent explosion. Another car pulled in and the older workman greeted the driver respectfully, took him aside and talked to him quietly, pointing to Frank. Nick sat in the pick-up, smoking and listening to a transistor radio. Frank watched the cameraman kneel on the earth where his mother's stomach would be, aiming his camera at the ruined headstone.

"Hey— !" Frank took a step toward him. The man who had been talking to the old workman came over straightening his tie, offered his hand, introduced himself. Frank raised on his toes to look over the man's shoulder.

"He shouldn't do that— "

The man released Frank's hand, looked puzzled. He turned around. The cameraman was walking toward the jumble of markers under the willow. Frank hurried over to his parents' grave. There were shallow footprints and he knelt and tried to smooth them over. Ants crawled over his fingers. The man followed him and said he was terribly sorry.

Frank wanted to hit something. "Jesus, why would he do that— ?"

The man shrugged, not understanding. "Who knows? It's the times, everything all . . . Kids— " He shrugged again. "Why kill the swans, eh?"

Frank thought of his mother emptying the brown paper bag over the water and he felt sick. "I didn't know that," he said.

The man nodded, described the way the old workman had found the bodies, said the old man was crying when he called to tell him about it. Frank saw, with terrible clarity, the old man bending over the dead birds, lifting them tenderly, saw the long necks drooping and no longer white. His stomach roiled. The man patted his arm, repeated that he was sorry. More people had come now and Frank heard the murmur of their voices, a question threading through the sound. The police kept them back. He heard a woman groan; she had probably come to visit one of the graves, was not just curious, attracted by the activity. He didn't know why he could tell that from the groan, but he could. The cameraman came over and asked Frank if he could get a picture. Frank listened to the woman sobbing and wondered which grave she belonged to. He let himself be led to the damaged stone and the cameraman told him to look down and would he mind taking off his glasses. The cameraman tried to adjust Frank's arms—

Frank let himself be posed, trying to see the woman, and then pushed the cameraman away. "You keep your goddamn feet off here," he said. The cameraman looked startled, then shrugged. Frank walked away and the morning was an instant brighter as the cameraman took another picture.

He went over to the policeman with the clipboard who was talking to the superintendent. He heard the policeman say something like " . . . Need somebody in the bull-pen . . . relief pitching is zilch now . . . " The superintendent smiled, nodded, opened his mouth to answer, but the policeman put his hand on the man's arm and glanced at Frank. "Yes, Mr. Warren?" He peeked at his clipboard for the name. The polite question seemed practiced, not his natural voice.

Frank wanted to ask him what he was going to do about the damage, almost said that he paid taxes. "Do you need me anymore?" The policeman said no and the superintendent again said he was sorry. As Frank walked away he heard the young officer laugh quietly and he cringed. His mouth trembled. He pushed his way through the small crowd and saw an old woman leaning on a young man in slacks and a windbreaker, crying. The young man's face was expressionless as he held the old woman against his chest and absently patted her shoulder. He was trying to see what was happening by the graves. Someone tugged at Frank's arm and said, "Hey, man, what happened?" Frank pulled his arm free and hurried to his car. He kept his head down and noticed there were grass stains on his knees. He had difficulty getting his car out to the road because other cars were wedged in at angles around him. He remembered that the pick-up, the police cars—they had all driven on the grass right up near the graves.

On the way home he cried, scrubbing his eyes with the heel of his hand. He kept seeing the holes where the stones had been ripped out and that was mixed with the memory of the day his mother was buried. He remembered very clearly someone saying it was a bad day for a funeral and how stupid that sounded and the light rain making the willow sag behind the sheened humps of the umbrellas on the other side of the grave and the minister—none of the family knew him—talking about Mrs. Warren's many friends while there were so few people. He pulled over to the curb and wept until his throat ached. A boy in a faded t-shirt stopped and bent over, staring at him with open mouth through the window on the passenger's side. Embarrassed, Frank started the engine.

Lena said, "My God!" and then kept interrupting him to say that the city was a terrible place and the garbage was piling up and the police couldn't do anything but write tickets and it was getting like a jungle. She kept asking him what the scene had looked like and she said they should move out of the city. Frank said he was going back to the cemetery; she looked at him and asked what for and he said he should do something and she said not to be silly, there was nothing he could do. He sat at the kitchen table, remembering snippets of the Old Man and his mother and he heard Lena on the telephone telling someone about hoodlum gangs smashing tombstones and writing filthy words and driving motorcycles over the graves.

He said, "Lena, for god's sake— " and she shushed him with a hand holding a cigarette, tracing cabalistic smoke designs in the air. He went outside and walked around the block, furious that everything seemed so normal, that traffic moved as it always did, and when he came back she was still on the phone. She covered the mouthpiece and said "Janet" silently. He tried to take the phone from her, but she swiveled away and talked for three more minutes, saying, " . . . Yes . . . *yes* . . . like a jungle . . . " and when he finally got the phone he didn't know what to say. Janet asked if he had let Ernie and Lou know and, when he said no, she said he should have done that right away. Janet started to cry and he felt tears in his own eyes. He squeezed his eyes tight. Janet told him to let her know what happened and he said he would. After he hung up, he wondered what that meant.

Louie kept saying, "I can't believe it." He told Frank to keep him posted, to make sure and let him know what happened and Frank promised he would. Ernie kept saying, "Oh, no," and then asked if there was insurance. Frank said he didn't know and Ernie said he'd better check on it first thing, that the cemetery probably had insurance to cover replacement of the stone and they'd better have because none of them had insurance to cover that kind of thing. Frank said he'd check on it and Ernie said he'd better take care of it right away, first thing in the morning at the latest, and to let him know what happened.

Frank stood by the front window, hands in his pockets. He remembered that after the Old Man died and they had gone down to the basement to divide the tools Ernie and Louie had argued over the cheap lathe and Ernie said maybe they should have the whole lot appraised, sell it, and divide the money equally. They hadn't done that—he couldn't remember why not—but he remembered that Ernie finally got the lathe. He squinted, trying to recall what he had taken. All he could remember was a shoebox of plans for bird houses, toys, lawn ornaments that revolved in the wind . . . he still had the box someplace.

Lena asked him what in the world he was doing tearing the closet apart and he said he was looking for something. When she asked him what, he said, "Just something." He found the box, tied with a shoe-lace, on the top shelf and took it into the bedroom. He spread the plans on the bed. The thick paper was grey and stiff with age and he couldn't remember the Old Man ever making any of the things. He put the plans carefully back in the box.

In the kitchen Lena was telling Sandy not to bother daddy because he had a lot on his mind, making it sound as if he had developed a mysterious disease. His daughter said, "O.K." without curiosity and Lena said, dangling an invitation for questions, " . . . now don't bother him because *something* happened today and he's very upset." He was enormously depressed, yet he wanted to hug Sandy for her bland, repeated "O.K." His daughter came into the living room and sprawled on the floor, wetting her fingertips and flipping the pages of the evening paper. He sat in his chair, tilting it back until the footrest popped up.

"Is it O.K. if I watch TV?"

He wanted to ask her to talk to him, but he didn't know how to start. "In a little while, honey," he said. He suddenly remembered why the tilted tombstones had seemed familiar. There was an illustration in one of Sandy's books. Ichabod Crane and the headless horseman were thundering past a cemetery and in the background, through the fog, tilted headstones appeared, each with a distorted human face. He'd read the story to her years ago and she giggled when he made his voice deep as he read, then, speaking naturally, put his finger on the picture and said, "—And look at the old spooky tombstones and *here's* old Ichabod racing through the graveyard and oh he's one scared fella," and she had giggled like a pot boiling.

From the kitchen Lena said, "Turn the TV on. There may be something— " giving the word eerie emphasis "—on the news" and he said "O.K.," not moving, watching his daughter. Lena ran water in the kitchen.

He said, "Sandy, do you remember your grandpa?"

"Sure," she said and he felt comforted.

"What do you remember about him?"

She had her elbows propped against bare thighs and her chin was in her palms. There was a scrape on one knee, the scab already wearing off, and he wondered when—how—she got that. She was studying the comic page unsmilingly. "Oh—he's kind of fat. But nice." She did not look up. "No, I mean your other grandpa." He waited, thinking she hadn't heard. "Sandy— ?" Lena stood in the kitchen door, her hands wrapped in a dishtowel. "Are you going to turn on the news?" He pulled the button on the set and Lena came in to sit on the sofa. Sandy started to say something and Lena told her to shhhh. There was nothing on the news about it and he didn't know whether he was sorry or not.

Lena woke up, disturbed by his twisting.
"I can't sleep," he said.
"You'd better have some milk," she said.
He told her, "You know, I've never made anything for Sandy. I can't remember ever, not once, making anything myself— "
She turned over and jammed her head in the pillow. She told him not to forget to put the milk away.
He took the box into the kitchen and spread the plans on the table, running his fingers over the stiff grey paper.

"Hon, she's an old lady. If we don't see her pretty soon, we may not get another chance." It's true. And, saying it, he believes it's true, but there is a comforting core of disbelief. In his gloomiest moments a tiny, vital part of him clings to a wistful optimism, the hope that the dead end is actually unfinished and someone has left a tiny crack he can squeeze through. To another dead end, equally incomplete. "What the hell, it's a chance to soak up a little sun— "

We splash through two days of unremitting rain, a constant weeping drizzle broken by sudden brief flashes of furious spatter raking the hood with fat silver explosions. Construction around Atlanta slows traffic to a creeping necklace of impatient metal; the wipers sluggishly drag themselves through a murky French grey film. The wipers need replacing, but if I mention it his shoulders will hunch. When the weather clears and I'm driving I'll have them changed. He'll say, "You didn't have to do that, hon. I was going to take care of it."

"You can tell from her note she's feeling pretty low. Just being in a hospital drags you down. Even if it's nothing serious, at her age— " His head sways dolefully at the lethal combination of age and hospitals. He gives me an unspoken glimpse of a frail figure clinging to life, sustained only by the promise of his arrival.

Crossing into Florida. Muggy, almost visible heat suffocates the rain. Ragged layers of slate and charcoal clouds race with us, rub each other, erase the occasional unreal swatches of blue.

His voice rises, the words coming quickly. I haven't refused and he knows now I won't refuse, but he wants something more, acceptance with enthusiasm. "On the way down maybe we could stop off, see the kids—oh, you know, take them out to dinner maybe, something like that. We'll get it over, that way we'll be on our own for the holidays— "

The long-sleeved pull-over, adequate in Georgia's morning chill, is a sticky sheath. I haven't told him about Alex yet. I was going to, am going to, but I haven't yet. No matter where I start it will be in the middle, there will be too many things left unsaid and we will have to trudge backwards, riffling through reasons. . . . Even if I simply blurt, "I'm in love with another man"—and I don't think I am—that wouldn't settle it. It's something he could understand, but he wouldn't accept, would resist with wounded stubbornness, ask why (and the very asking of that tiny question means there is no answer), recite a litany of the good things we have going for us, the good times we've had. He'll reel out a tangled line of his virtues, limp as wet wash and each lacerated by one of my faults—and I'll respond with my own soggy skein. In ten minutes Alex will be shoved out of sight and we'll be locked in our own history, arguing about who-promised-who-what, who said this, who *meant* that— then we will ride in sullen silence. It's so much easier to start with silence.

"Look— " the motor club map crackles in his hands. "We go down 75—good highway all the way—we can stop off at Gatlinburg— " for some inexplicable reason he thinks I harbor a secret wish to see Gatlinburg. I don't. It's another of those incomprehensible confusions like his certainty that I adore red scarves. "Take it easy—easy drive—be good for us to get away for a while, shake the old winter miseries. Kind of like a little vacation— " A vacation: visiting his children, his ancient aunt. A vacation should be brochures on slick paper, airlines, a few timeless hours suspended above water while plump clouds tease the windows and then the emergence somewhere else with strange words and coins and customs clerks.

He insists on stopping at the hospitality center. "That's the real thing, eh? Not like the canned stuff we get, eh?" Swirling the paper cone under his nose, he inhales deeply as though it's brandy, not tepid orange juice. He buys an ashtray studded with lacquered sea shells. "For the new office," he says casually, wanting to be praised, a little-boy look, the crayoned Mother's day card in a grubby hand.

Each evening we must make a decision: Holiday Inn (traditional; successors to the old New England coaching houses), Ramada, Quality Court, Days Inn (a creeping invasion from the South, angular kudzu vines). A bellboy, dollar-absorbing anachonism, strolls in front of the car and points to our room. We unload our own baggage. In the room with its twin floral bedspreads, blue-green carpet, twin prints of Sorrento on the beige walls, formica dresser bolted to the floor, television set bolted to the wall, orange swag lamps on chains—we don't know which we've chosen, have to check the matchbooks to find who shelters us. Before he unpacks, Paul collects all but one bar of soap, an hygienic journal of our passage. Photographs, postcards are obsolete; someday we can spread our little bars on the coffee table and say "Remember—?"

In a motel room somewhere in Kentucky. In the elastic moment before sleep. A coincidence of numbers, the flickering memory of shield-shaped highway markers: 75   75   75 . . . Paul is five years older, a gap that was secure before. Now he is five years older, but somehow the gap has narrowed. And we are, together, seventy-five years old! It is an incredible chest-freezing number and in the moment before sleep and sleep itself I am wide awake and frightened. Seventy-five years. I don't tell him about it (we no longer share the peculiar humor or horror of dreams); he would find nothing extraordinary in it. Or, worse, he would.

Alex might have stopped for orange juice, might have sniffed the paper cup with mock appreciation, would have offered me a gallant toast. He might have done the same things Paul did (with the added nicety of the toast) yet it would be totally different. But of course Alex wouldn't have suggested the trip in the first place.

I drive while he dozes. Florida has no width, is only a narrow strip of land on either side of the highway. The sun peeks out under the clouds, smearing their bottoms with opal glaze. The dark green orange groves seem stunted, have a hard wet glittering sheen. Mickey Mantle, spraddle-legged, grins out from sign after sign. The signs say Mickey lives in a trailer court. Behind the signs I feel there is nothing but a few more signs, squat orange trees, trailers huddled on the marshy plain like cattle and then the ocean.

Late in the afternoon, after we stop for coffee, we change places. He drives with a rocking motion, coming up to the limit, releasing the accelerator and letting the speed drop slightly, then easing his foot down again. It makes me slightly seasick. He stabs the silence with snatches of old songs, questions that demand no answers or even attention, serve only to reassure him that I'm in the car with him. "Would you like to live down here? I wouldn't. No way. Hot all the time, no hills, no anything. You see all those oranges? Frost, hell. It's just another rip-off. If you weren't crazy about golf you'd go crazy period. God, nothing to do all day but play golf. Think you'd like to live down here, hon? I sure wouldn't."

He plays golf occasionally, a matter of business. He laughs at his own lack of skill, talks about smashes into the rough, putts missed by that much. Alex plays tennis with controlled exuberance, a kind of economic frenzy, never taking it easy on a weaker opponent, never bemoaning a loss.

A scene burned into the memory, as vividly unforgettable, as something seen in a movie and retained in every detail. Late in the afternoon. On the right a shallow, weed-rimmed pond, the water dull brass stippled with silver. A single wide-spaced row of trees, some kind of pine with tall bare trunks and caps of bristly foliage, forms a gaunt columnade between highway and water; they shutter the sun in melancholy patterns of soft cathedral light and cool dark shadow. We swing out to pass a late-model Chevrolet moving at a doggedly conscientious 55. An old man, chinless chin rigid above a wattled neck, eyes glazed and frozen in a squint behind ocher-lensed glasses, hands locked on the wheel. His wife (no question: his wife) slumped beside him against her door, head thrown back, mouth open—asleep or dying, it could be either, is probably both. The

back seat is crammed with clothing, boxes, two lamps with irrepa-
rably squashed shades, a small television set staring out the back
window at a Hertz U-Haul nosing the rear bumper. In the sad
golden late afternoon light they are moving to Florida in their
golden years. A startled bird rises from the water beyond them, ris-
ing on a veil of irridescent water droplets, a fragile fountain spray, a
shimmering fan that captures the Chevrolet. The scene is
frozen . . . no, not frozen; that's too cold. Simply *there* in the
hazed Poussin light of late afternoon. It makes me inexpressibly
sad. If I went back in a year, in ten years, at that precise place I
would pass the old couple and the bird, the transparent curtain of
water, the ineffably nostalgic light, the Chevrolet eternally moving
to Florida and the golden years.

   Maxine, Paul's ex-wife, answers the phone. I can hear her part of
the conversation in his responses. He isn't sure what tone he should
use with me in the room and settles for polite, fictitious formality.
Maxine is, as always, informally cheerful. Their divorce was acri-
monious, they tore themselves apart in bitter biting confusion, as
physically painful as wrenching apart the edges of an unhealed
wound. Gradually, predictably, they've mellowed toward each
other and now they're comfortable-old-friendish, a relationship
that makes Paul feel guilty toward me.
   Don and I, two young but mature and rational adults, split
amicably, put the decision in reasonable, mutually consoling words
over bad margaritas at a little pseudo-Spanish restaurant, one of
those obscure "our place" places with wrought-iron grills and
styrofoam oak beams latticing the ceiling. There's no reason why we
can't be friends. We walked back to the apartment hand in hand.
We keep in touch (there's no reason why we can't be friends): Don
faithfully sends me birthday cards, the large cruel cartoon kind with
snappy exclamation-pointed statements on the ravages of age; I
mail him religious Christmas cards (from the less-expensive, for-
people-we-owe-but-don't-particularly-care-for stack) signed Mr.
and Mrs. Paul Fauss. Don hasn't remarried and someone said he'd
been living with a perennial graduate student for a couple of years.

The someone said the woman probably has a thyroid condition because "she has eyes like a sick lemur."

Maxine is telling Paul the kids aren't home yet. "Kids" is a silly but unsubstitutable term; Stephen is enrolled in the local junior college, Marie is seventeen and finishes high school in a few months. Maxine is saying she's sure the kids will be delighted to go to dinner and she wants to know if we'd like to stop by for a cocktail. Paul says that would be nice (rolling his eyes at me to show what a hopeless chatterer she is), but we're on kind of a tight schedule and we just checked in and have to clean up.

Maxine is a good housekeeper. She periodically sends snapshots of the kids posed smiling under the Christmas tree, smiling from the living room sofa, smiling from the patio, the family room. I pretend to glance at the pictures and scrutinize the backgrounds, searching for signs of disarray. I know that Maxine has a passion for glass figurines of owls. All the furniture seems to be highly polished.

Before he hangs up he asks, "How are you?" his voice subtly different, the formality melting, and I know she tells him she's fine in that madonna contralto she'll always have; a voice like that is a froggy curse at fifteen and a delight forever after.

Oh so casually he turns his back to me, makes the conversation private, says, "that's good—" pause "—fine. Oh, a headache now and then, that kind of thing—" pause "—Oh, she's fine, too. Right." When he puts the receiver down he will slap his hands together, be paternally jovial, will ask where I want to eat as though we are familiar with the local spots. When the tension between us is at a low ebb our most animated discussions are about food. I don't like to cook; Paul's sole contribution is the concoction of salad dressings. The refrigerator has one shelf devoted to jelly jars half-filled with blended mixtures of cheese, beer, sour cream, horse-radish, ketchup, mayonnaise, yogurt and a variety of vinegars. Lime-green furry cultures grow on the jars in the rear. We eat out four or five times a week and each excursion is prefaced with a debate: what should we have, is it worth driving outside the city, do you feel like that, we had that last week. We usually settle for Villa Capri (Italian), The Capri Lounge (Greek) or Mel's Steak & Chop

Palace Entertainment Nitely (no chops on the menu, no Mel on the premises, a piano bar). We talk a great deal about food. If we went on water diets the silence would drown us.

He is flipping through the telephone book, running his fingers down the restaurant columns. He has slapped his hands, asked the question, heard me say I need a bath before I can even think of food. That disappoints him, but he recovers.

"Can I come in?"
The water is cooling. Years of shared nakedness bring familiarity. He sits on the john seat, scrunched and benign brown nubbin of his sex limply staring down at its reflection in the water. Alex is never completely flaccid, always threatens, has the latent promise of arousal, carries a miniature python with a half-digested meal slung low in a roan thicket.

"How's Maxine?" The rim of the tub is soothingly cold on my neck, my toes protrude from the water, wrinkled and white.

He studies his hands, wary. If neutral, he will sound cold. If warm, it will sound as if he is still fond of her (he is, of course, and feels guilty about it, feels it is disloyal. He must often make comparisons between us; it's only natural. His shins are hairless, look as if they've been shaved. It seems an odd place to go bald. Don had luxuriantly furred calves, left the bed sheets and bath tub sprinkled with worm-like filaments . . . but perhaps by now he, too, has glossy shins), will worry that I'm jealous of their friendship. I will be. I am, in a generalized, nonhostile way. He opts for a slanting heartiness. "Oh, fine. She's fine. Max's business is going real well." For eight years Maxine has been married to one Max Durcott, a plumbing and heating specialist of chilling amiability. "She says the weather's been really something. Warm, lots of sun. Really something."

"Micky's probably brown as a berry." My toes move back and forth.

"Who—? Oh, yeah!" He blesses the comment with laughter, a grunting humor. He watches his fingers mate. "I was just thinking—hon, if you want to skip this thing with the kids, I mean, it's O.K." He doesn't want me to skip it, is not really sure what he wants. He'll be uncomfortable at every reference to Maxine, will slide his eyes at me if I ask Marie how her mother is, will hastily change the subject and so give it emphasis. But he wants me there. What he would like best is for us to be one happy family. Maxine and I, he and Max, the kids. Tonight he would be content if I go along, but deaf as a post. More and more I talk to myself in cliches; getting long in the tooth.

Is this the time to say: fine, you go ahead? I think I'll have room service send something up and after I eat I'll give Alex a call. Why Alex? Darn it, I've had so many things on my mind . . . didn't I mention it, Paul? Alex and I are: intimate (lashes coyly flapping); . or: carrying on a passionate affair (nostrils flared, proud breasts rosy-nippled, heaving above the water); or: shacking (tough broad, lip curled). It's not the time. Naked in mine bath, I don't know which pose to strike.

He doesn't know what he wants so he forges on, trying to get me to commit myself so he can react. "I mean, I know the trip's been a grind for you so far."

My palm deposits a sudsy blot on his thigh. "Trying to get rid of me? Would you rather I didn't go?" We are bound by gelatin, scramble to find places on a tiny island of mush. All answers are questions.

"Aw, hell, hon, no, that's not what I meant." It is too brusque, forcefully defensive because a part of him (but only a part) means exactly that.

"Of course I'll go, Paul. Family's important to you." Now he has to press me for something more, attendance by desire not duty. He surprises me, pulls his eyebrows together deepening the ruts in his forehead, accepts the decision however flawed. He says O.K. without inflection, repeats it with vigor.

"Let's get dolled up, eh? Show the kids we're not over the hill." The laugh is supposed to show he is joking, shows clearly he isn't. "Got anything special in mind you want to eat?"

I pretend to consider it, letting the water kiss my chin. "No, nothing special."

"Well, we can let the kids decide. They should be calling back pretty soon, as soon as one of them gets in. They probably know every cheapo place around here.'' He will insist on someplace expensive and, later, will feel guilty about the extravagance, will express amazement at the size of the bill, will make sure I note he had the $7.95 prime rib instead of the $8.95 steak and will resent both the sacrifice and the need to apologize.

His buttocks flex, form soft hollows as he goes to answer the phone. Beneath the chemically saturated water my skin is the dead white of magnolia blossoms, hip and thigh flesh flattens on the tub bottom, looks spongey. I'm becoming a loose woman.

"This is a nice place. Umm mmm, a nice place." He drapes an arm over the back of his chair, spends too much time examining the red-flocked paper, the oils which are endless variations of blankly handsome matadors swirling crimson capes above wicked horns and sooty-haired women with ridiculously firm, polished, apple-smooth breasts flouncing to guitars. Each picture has its own light, all have vibrant yet curiously flat colors. He turns back to us, knots his fingers on the table, takes a deep breath and plunges into the initial tension. "Now remember, nobody looks at the right side of the menu, right?" He laughs too hard trying to escalate their polite smiles, avoids my eyes. "So—how've you been?" The question is so vague, so predictable there can only be one vague predictable answer.

"Fine," Stephen says and Marie's "fine" is only a tick behind, an echo. She makes up for it by bobbing her sleek head and adding, "Just fine. How about you?"

"Oh, fine, fine." A pause. "So—how's school going?"

His children *(their* children) are stunningly unexceptional and so normal they have individual charm. Stephen has his father's eyes, a warm chocolatey brown, like maple cremes; the bridge of his nose, too, is very thin, highly arched, making his eyes seem too close together. His mouth is Maxine's, narrow upper lip sharply indented below the nostrils. Smiling. Marie's shoulders are a boney yoke, form a gentle u; she hasn't yet learned to handle her height and, even sitting, tries to minimize herself. Eventually she'll surrender, explode into Maxine's pneumatic roundness, but now she's almost gaunt. She is acutely conscious of a trio of red splotches, a pulsating constellation blooming on her cheek and awkwardly poses so that she can cover them with her fingers. They aren't really that obvious, but to her they must feel as large as walnuts, fiery hot beacons. I itch to pull her fingers away, to tell her to forget them and relax. Stephen, unaccustomed to the necktie, has centered the knot so often it is a squashed lump of indigo cloth.

They were resentful at first. The divorce was an intrusion on their stable base, a demand they come out of self-absorbed shells and notice the old folks are alive and kicking. And of course they were confused: how can you heap righteous hatred on parents who divide. Except for an inevitable uncertainty at each meeting we get along fine now. For some reason they are more comfortable with me than with Paul. Perhaps because I don't cajole them into loving me. Once a year they dutifully visit and, by the end of each visit, Marie has doled out a year of secrets and Stephen is treating me as an older sister (an occasional incestuous gleam in his chocolatey eyes the last few years that amuses, flatters and, finally, depresses). It's difficult to know what they really feel about us; probably not much one way or the other. They diplomatically discuss Max the plumber in neutral tones. Are they that circumspect talking about Paul and me when they're on familiar territory at home? I suspect we really exist for them only when they see us.

"How's—Max?" There is always a tiny skip when he mentions Max, a hesitation in choosing a name. "Max" sounds too familiar; "your step-father" too cold; "your mother's husband" both clumsy and unintentionally sarcastic.

"Oh, he's fine." Marie blushes furiously, moves her water glass in arabesques on the table cloth. Her shoulders threaten to meet. "Just fine."

"He had a cold," Stephen blurts and looks uncomfortable at granting Max this individuality.

"Oh, that's too bad. That's a real shame." Paul is too sincerely concerned, seizes this frailty too eagerly. "Lots of it around this year. We've had five or six people out every week. God, if it wasn't for Manpower . . . Of course we've got all that cold weather. But there's a hell of a lot of it around this year. We haven't had it yet, have we, hon?" He always tries too hard to include me, to show how close we are, how all decisions are mutual, the result of loving consultation. When Stephen and Marie are with us he always carefully holds my chair and coat, opens the car door.

I pat his entwined fingers and hear my voice, too bright, a half-octave too high. "Not a sniffle. Down here with all the healthy orange juice we'll probably both catch it." I wonder if they can detect the parody of cooing wife. I don't want them to think there is any strain between Paul and me because I don't want them balancing us against Max and Maxine. Why? I don't know.

Or maybe I do. Paul isn't afflicted with profundity . . . no that isn't really true. Everyone has a moment or two of insight, the passage through the mind of something profound, a glimpse of something strange and true. Or at least true for him, at that moment. Maybe it can't be put into words, not adequate words, but it comes to everyone. If we're wise we hurry on to something else. Paul has his moments. We ride for hours in "companionable silence," that ghastly euphemism couples use when they no longer have anything to say to each other. And I know that unless I'm sleeping the mind isn't thoughtless: plans, large and small, the indulgence in private fantasies, conversations re-enacted and re-arranged so that one is witty. Something passes through the mind. So I know that when we're riding in companionable silence his mind isn't a blank either, something is churning in his head. Of course we don't spout deep thoughts at each other (or even trivial thoughts). We used to try, but not any more.

Anyway, once, gropingly, half to himself as though embarrassed, he said he thought we (a broad "we" meant to include everyone but at the same time a very personal you-and-I we and an even more personal "me" we)—he said we become what others think we are. I don't remember what preceded the silence that preceded that statement. Probably we were talking about something he did or failed to do. Anyway, even more hesitantly, as if feeling his way, he said the pain of failure isn't so much in the failing; that can be overcome, might even help. But failing communicates something about us to people and they judge us by it, form an image of us and, in watching and hearing them, we see that image and shape ourselves to the reflection. Even if we don't want to, even if we loathe it, we believe what we see.

I don't remember if I said anything to that. I don't think so. But I believe he may have laid claim on his profundity, the discovery of a small, vital truth. And so I don't want Marie and Stephen thinking, "She's getting old and witchy."

"Guess who's got a big promotion?" He says it with gusto, meaning to tantalize. They turn to me expectantly. Who else at the table got a big promotion? Would Paul promote himself?

"Paul—" the exasperation in my voice sounds false, coy, cute-spousish.

"Go on, tell 'em, hon." His smile is a wide slash of childish delight. His arm snakes around my shoulder and, under my chin, his shirt cuff is damp with sweat, smells slightly sour. "She's going to manage her own office. How about that? Old Alex isn't going to get to chase her around the desk every day now, is he, hon?" I cannot see his eyes. "Alex—" he doesn't explain who Alex is; they lack the curiosity to interrupt and ask "—figures why should he settle for half the money in town when he can have it all. And he can recognize a good sharp operator when he has one." The arm constricts, the hug is—affectionate? inexorable? "He's opening a branch over in Wilton Mall and guess who's going to be honcho?"

There are moments with him when I'm suddenly dipped in cold water, when the eyes of the mind pop open in shock at the suspicion I've underestimated him, that his smile is more than a bland exposure of teeth, that his subtlety is deep and immense, that he conceals cold incalculable reaches where something scaled and dark and infinitely patient, infinitely unforgiving watches and waits. There are those moments but they quickly pass. Perhaps it's just wishful thinking, a need to give him angles and curves where there are only flat planes.

Stephen is saying hey, that's great, with spurious enthusiasm; Marie offers congratulations. Both try very hard—and I'm moved by the effort— to convey the impression they're impressed. But they aren't. Neither really knows or cares what "business" is, both are convinced it's something boring people do. Stephen's ambition, if so squirmingly elusive a goal can be pinned down with "ambition," is to eventually take a liberal arts degree and "get into the ecology thing, like with what Exxon and General Motors are doing and Ralph Nader, stuff like that, you know?" I don't know and it irritates me because it's been such a short time since I thought I knew. Marie's plans are less precise than her brother's.

Anything I say will be too much for them and annoyingly insufficient for me so I give them a minute or two of my imagine-little-old-me-doing-such-a-thing and mention Waylon Jennings to change the subject. Stephen is immediately animated, informative, a burbling fountain of liner notes; Marie is disdainful—she's "into" jazz and the red splotches momentarily forgotten, she offers counterquotes, sighs over Kai Winding. She pronounces it "Kay."

Paul pretends confusion, says that Crosby was the last of the good singers although Buddy Clark was tremendous, draws giggles and groans from his children with his imitation of Perry Como.

Stephen, drained of album data, shows he's an adult, concerned with adult matters. "Are you going to see Aunt Grace?"

"Oh, sure. That's the main reason we came down. Right, hon?"

"She's pretty rocky." Stephen wags his head sadly. "To have your leg cut off, oh, wow—"

Paul is shocked; he didn't know about that, regrets the loss and, more, his ignorance of the loss. "Oh, no! God, I didn't know that. I thought she was just in for a general check-up, rheumatism, something like that. Her last letter didn't say—Aw, no—" as if by stout denial he will negate fact.

"Mom was down there Sunday—" Stephen tortures his tie. "She'll be okay. She's something, she really is."

Whenever Aunt Grace is mentioned—Auntgrace is a single word—it is always with wry admiration. Oh, Aunt Grace is hard to get along with sometimes. But she's something. She's a tough old bird. But she's something. Sometimes she says things that really zing you (pause, a rueful shake of the head) . . . but she's something, she really is. That admiring qualification must always be appended because Aunt Grace has managed to survive and age somehow mitigates faults. Someone younger would be bitchy; Aunt Grace is crusty, testy—and she's really something. Think of it: Aunt Grace is in her nineties, but her mind is sharp as a razor. Translated, this means her tongue is stropped by time to the keenest edge. Aunt Grace is the family institution. Gradually, one every two years or so, then with a rush, Paul's relatives have wrapped themselves around trees while driving under the influence, have inhaled fatal germs, surrendered to hypertension and decayed lungs, fallen down basement steps and one (dear dotty Uncle Felix, he of the hideous ties and scalding breath) was shot in Baltimore because two sixteen-year-olds found his wallet with only four dollar bills, a driver's license, social security card and a tattered clipping of a James Reston article an insult to their desperado initiative, a slap at their expenditure of time. Through the years various nephews simply died.

Now Aunt Grace is the only bulwark between Paul and the ominous distinction "oldest living member of the family." When she goes he dreads taking her place, assuming her inevitably fatal position. And, too, Aunt Grace stretches into so much of his past, is a repository of so many memories. When she dies they, too, will die. They exchange sporadiç, unaffectionate letters (Aunt Grace's a triumphant litany of contemporaries who have "passed on, poor dear"; Paul's a recital of cars purchased, weather reports, remember-when references to his mother and father, the house on Van Buren, summers spent on the farm in Iowa). His letters have been longer and more frequent the last few years.

I have a brace of cousins in Seattle and we trade Christmas cards with notes penned on the back insisting, without conviction, we should get together. We wouldn't know each other if we met.

"Well, we'll take her something, maybe some candy. Okay, hon?"

"Oh, of course," as though taking candy to Aunt Grace will make everything all right, a confectionary amalgam of penicillin and chicken soup to keep her alive a while longer, will prop her between him and the future.

"It's the alternator," Stephen says judiciously. The car has been threatening to do something—or, more accurately, not do something—for weeks and Paul promised he would have it thoroughly

checked before we left. He has either forgotten or, more likely
assumed/hoped the problem would take care of itself. He has an un-
shakeable faith that mechanical things will simply run when they're
asked to, is always angrily bewildered when they don't. And so lawn
mowers, oil reservoirs arid, lock in rebellion, unsharpened saws and
bits tear and gouge. If I say I'll take care of them he bristles with
resentment, unhappy survivor of a tradition that assumed males
were, by some preternatural instinct, handy.

He curses General Motors and stops twisting the ignition key,
slaps his hands together, insists he told the garage people to check
the whole thing over (the very intensity, the righteousness, of his in-
dignation tells me he did no such thing), goes back into the
restaurant to call a repairman.

"Poor dad," Stephen says with a smug look of sympathy.

Alex is competent. The working of engines neither awes nor fasci-
nates him. If necessary, he can manage minor repairs, but he avoids
it by having his gadgets regularly tended by experts. He doesn't feel
his masculinity threatened if he has to consult someone trained to
handle a problem, does not pretend either interest in or knowledge
of technical explanations, simply describes symptoms in lucid terms
and expects things to be fixed. They are and his car, knockless,
squawkless, always moves when he wants it to.

He hasn't suggested marriage, let alone a divorce. He was married, mentions it casually, without bitterness, regret or nostalgia. He
hasn't suggested marriage, but hasn't insisted marriage is out of the
question. If my situation changes, perhaps he will change. In what
way?

"Mechanical things seem to hate him," Marie says, trying to be
loyal.

From the motel pool we can look across to the beach where college kids trudge, dissolving and reforming in little groups. Frisbees
and gulls trace looping patterns on the sky. A number of tanned
lean-hipped young men walk hand in hand.

Paul's hair is thick, crinkly, mattress-stuffing grey. On his soft
chest the hair is a wet scraggly T. He seems to be melting in the heat,
something inside seeping away as the inner core collapses. His

breasts are loose, pendulous, increasingly female. A frightening myth: people begin to look like each other after they've lived together. They don't really. It's simply aging's androgynous process. One of the few facts retained from Biology 102: the worm *Grubea protandrica* (the name precisely wedged in the memory, another of those useless unerasable snippets like the capital of Guam is Agana or the state motto of Idaho is "Let It Be Forever") is male in autumn and winter, female in spring, neuter in summer. Paul (and I?) lie heavy in our dying summer. Do people really start to look like each other after living together? God, that's a ghastly notion. How would the body know which way to go? I mean, Don and I. Then Paul and I. Paul and Maxine, Paul and I, Max and Maxine . . . we shall gather in the warm twilight, each a plump droop-breasted duplicate of the other.

His sun-glasses have mirrored lenses so that I see the girl sway behind me, aggressive indented mound clearly outlined, thrusting against the tight sulphur-yellow suit below the belly, navel winking as she moves. Her ribs are cinnamon-tinted satin. Paul's stomach contracts, squeezing out oily liquid ridges between the folds of dangerously pinkening skin. She flows across the silver surface of his glasses and I know his eyes move with her.

"How you feeling, hon?"

"Fine." I close my eyes and watch flamingo-rimmed green shapes move on the lids.

"That's good." He lets his stomach relax. "You want a drink or something?"

"Mmm-mmm."

"You want me to get you a sandwich or something? A salad maybe?"

"No, I'm fine."

"O.K. You want something, let me know, O.K.?" He has been irritatingly solicitous since the car conked out, wants me to forget the image of the repairman wiping his hands on a greasy cloth, would like to trot off to get me something, a slice of expiation on toasted white impaled by a toothpick wrapped in shiny transparent paper. He would always like things to start from scratch.

This would be the time to say something, to tell him that when we get home we don't have to unpack, that one set of suitcases will be going someplace else. With the sun breathing wet pressure on my stomach, pushing tension out, it would be a fine time to tell hm that I'm leaving, without rancor, just because not staying may be easier than staying.

And there would be a crinkling of the eyes behind the mirrors, an expression of pain and surprise when another mechanical thing functions strangely. I would see myself in the mirrors and eyes. "But why, hon? Things will work out. Why?" A childish whine, questioning an adult's irrational behavior. There aren't any solid answers, no single simple explanations. Mention of Alex would only bring more questions and Alex isn't a reason. Alex probably isn't even important here. Paul, I'm just tired of being depended on.

"Maybe I'll have a daiquiri."

"Hey, great. Sounds good. Don't go away." He pinches my arm. Eyes closed, I listen to the slap of his rubber thongs on the tiles moving away.

I'm just tired of being depended on.

"Are you asleep, hon?" His whisper and hand creep across the bed. He has been lying awake, watching the sulphur-yellow bikini undulate on the dark ceiling, the air conditioner's moist throb echoing the rhythm of the winking navel. His solitary movements are a parody of a courting dance. He tries to sleep; then a sequence of shifts and flops, a shuddering sigh to signal his wakefulness, to make me ask what's wrong. An attempt to seduce by telepathy. Eyes scrunched shut in concentration, he silently spells the words, going from an innocuous SEX to a fervent FUCK, sharpening the letters, trying to force them into my head. When that fails he begins to twitch, turning from side to side, annoyed by my absolute stillness. More sighs. Lying on my side, back to him, a stone, I follow the progress of his passion. I can tell the precise moment when his fingers stalk his thigh, curl to capture himself, when sensation and control are in balance and his hand gently strokes the same image he is framing in his mind. Over the air conditioner's hum, through the double-paned windows, a shriek of laughter, muted, spatters the room. One of the kids has been stirred from lethargy. The laughter is high-pitched, may be male or female. They come by habit now; the vernal pilgrimage to Ft. Lauderdale part of a mythic process. They will go home and lie about the great time they had. They prowl Atlantic Boulevard, sleeveless jerseys a uniform, snapping the hair away from their eyes. Refugees, not revelers.

The laughter, the dull fluctuating glow of flashers on patrolling police cars a cold blue beat on the windows where the draperies gap, an awareness of bodies moving outside or sitting like ranks of oddly plumed birds—these destroy the sense of privacy, make this strange room among strangers something erotic. There is communicable excitement and desperation in the air. The slither of his hand against the sheets, the tentative insinuation of his fingers at my spine's base, the dry taste of the pillow clamped between my teeth . . . "Hon? Are you awake?"

Whatever else he is, Alex is not a leaner. Alex would not depend on me.

Aunt Grace is an intruder on the wide bed, a lumpy disruption. Her body cannot accommodate itself to the mechanical demands, not even whittled down. The bed was designed to fit a space, not a person; it arches where she does not bend.

Orderlies, blue-smocked, are dark-skinned. The interns are dark-skinned blurs above white coats. Nurses trade rapid Spanish, reluctantly shift into heavily accented English when strangers come into their world. Their politeness is a barrier, the sound of their laughter in the halls curls around the bed.

"We've been a very good patient," the nurse says perfunctorily. "Very" has no "y," trails off in slurred r's. Saucy face, breasts an impertinent thrust, bottom a tight rolling rage against the uniform's restrictions, her vitality is too much for the room. Paul tries not to notice her, tries not to let me see him noticing her. The nurse has large perfect teeth, terribly white between plum lips. "We've been very good." Before, Aunt Grace would have automatically, scathingly rebelled against that collective inanity. At least she would have glared. Now she lies with hair grey, damp, her face wrinkled and grey. It is a shrunken old man's face, eyelids tissue-thin, eyes swallowed by smudged bluish-green circles. She is excruciatingly thin but her cheeks are puffy as though she is hiding something there. The plastic wristband is heavy as a chain on her wrist. A sticky whiteness leaks from the corners of her mouth, dries in small scaly patches. A welter of Kleenex on the tub-stand beside the bed. An unread book. A plastic hairbrush, its bristles free of hair. A papier-mache pot of burnt orange and copper flowers sticking up from a nest of ferns.

Paul doesn't know what to say, gently touches her hand as though afraid it might shatter. He wants to stay, to say something miraculous, wants to go.

"How are you, Aunt Grace? You're looking good. She really looks good, doesn't she, hon?" Aunt Grace's cheeks, raddled bellows, swell and collapse but she doesn't say anything. Her eyelids roll up slowly and even more slowly slide down. The window blinds are open but the glass is tinted an ugly blue-brown so that only light and dark are discernible. Rain would be noticed. Whether it's sunny or cloudy it's impossible to tell.

On the other end of the room a fat woman whimpers and shifts, gingerly caresses the dressing replacing a breast, sleeps exuding a smell of toilet water and medicine and body. The smell is exactly that of cream cheese appetizers left out too long.

As we leave he is still clutching the box of candy. He gives it to a nurse at the desk who says "Gracias," then says "thank you" with an impersonal smile and no feeling. She puts the box out of sight somewhere around her knees. Are there dozens of boxes down there, the chocolate turning chalky white with heat and age? A question for elementary math students: how many nurses would it take to eat all the candy left by all the—?

Moving north the heat is stripped away, the painful blue of sky dilutes. We do not stop for orange juice at the border.

Will Alex think I tumbled into bed simply to get the office? Possibly. Does that bother me? Oh, yes. We are what others think we are.

The flat has a sodden sound, a wet flump-flump-flump. Paul has a full head of hair, but allows his tires to go bald. And there is no spare. Of course there is no spare. Of all the things I asked him to check, I didn't remember to ask him if he put the spare back when he vacuumed the trunk. He worries that I'm angry, feels abused, doesn't think it's his fault. I'm not angry. If I don't hold my face rigid I'll laugh and that would crush him. The air is chill. A cool Tennessee mist rises from beneath the bridge. Dogwoods are ghostly shapes on the twilighted hills.

"I'm sorry." And he is. If he weren't sorry he wouldn't be Paul. But not sorry enough ever to change. If he were that sorry he wouldn't be Paul.

Large mosquito-like insects with filmy wings dance on the windshield like brown snowflakes. Trucks round the curve, rock the car with the fury of their passing, roar into the mist with mocking red lights. He looks forlorn, thumb raised, shoulders hunched, walking slowly backward away from me. Trucks buffet him and he sways, blending into the mist.

I run the motor, play the radio. I'll have to leave twenty minutes earlier to get over to Wilton.

Hours later he returns in the cab of a pick-up truck. A young man with huge ears and too little chin bounces a tire on the highway, competently changes the tire, overcharges us. "You should always carry a spare," he says and Paul nods.

"Hon, I'm sorry, I really am." He is over the speed limit. 'Hey, look. We'll stop in the next town, find a room and then go out and get something to eat, eh?" The greenish glow from the dashboard lights coats his face. "Hon, it's going to be O.K.," an immense adhesive slapped over innumerable wounds.

"All right."

"Hon—" he takes a deep breath, waiting for the words to come, settles for, "I'm sorry."

"I'd like some Mexican food."

"Hey, you would? That's great!" His green face, the smile pale emerald, turns briefly. "That really sounds good. Remember that place we went in Cincinnati? God, that seems like a hundred years ago. Remember? The guitar player? Those big shrimp? We've had some good times, you know?"

There is no Mexican food. He hunches over the directory in the booth, trots back to the car. "How about Italian?" The Villa Naples is closed. We wind up eating at an International House of Pancakes.

"Tomorrow night it'll be different," he says and means it. "I don't care what happens, tomorrow night you get Mexican food."

A Simple Woman

Everyone knew Annie . . .

Small towns don't need bogeymen; there is always the known and solid threat: if you don't eat that I'll call Pee Pee Bonnard and *he'll* make you eat it. Or: just look at your hands. They're filthy. You look just like Dirty Lucas. Do you want to look like Lucas? Terrible and effective threats.

. . . and everyone knew exactly what kind of woman she was.

If they didn't come straight home after watching Gregory Peck in *The Keys of the Kingdom* or Van Heflin in *Tap Root* at the Rialto, if they stopped at Sanderson's Drug Store to giggle confidences, daughters would be told: you're going to wind up just like Annie. But this was a rare, meaningless threat; the daughters knew they were not like Annie and would not wind up like her.

Years later, in another, larger town with no familiar monsters to terrify his own children he would, for no apparent reason, clearly remember—among other things—bright edgeless slices of Saturday mornings, would remember seeing her in one of the taverns on Bridge Street, Saloon Alley as it was called, the half-mile stretch between the C&EI tracks and the small houses that gradually became bigger, more expensive until you came to the queer lightning-rodded turrets, curved porches, contorted wooden scallops of the Adler House. Beyond the Adler House, fifty yards to the south, the town ended in a metal rectangle punctuated with .22 holes. The sign, when you went around it and looked back, said TUSCOMA pop.

10,032. Beyond that, miles of straight flat road sliced through corn fields.

She would be in Bardulli's or the Kozy Korner or Sivet's but most often in the Happy Cat. Never in the Silver Dollar or Green's Lounge or Durban's.

The Happy Cat, the Korner, Sivet's, Bardulli's—to the boy they were bewilderingly the same: the same yellowish brown dimness; the same high dark bar on the left running from the cigar case near the entrance to the smudged white cooler; the same tall fat bottle of sausages sulking in greasy liquid on the bar; the same line of encrusted spitoons; the same three or four plain wooden tables and straight-backed chairs on the right; the same saw-dusty wooden floors that caught your dull footsteps and bounced the sound up to high ceilings lined with embossed metal, rolled the sound back through the doorway leading to the single toilet; the same peculiar moist and not unpleasant smell of beer, smoke, and the odor of fried fish that lingered from Friday night to Friday night.

And the question was always the same: "You sure you didn't collect already?" The boy would bob his head, offer to show the man behind the bar his receipt book. In Durban's or the Silver Dollar there were never any questions except "how much I owe you?"; he would always say, "twenty-five cents."

In the Happy Cat the bartender wore a plaid shirt, faded, sleeves rolled up crimping thick white arms. He would say, "I don't know, now, fella was in here last night, I remember. Looked like you 'nough to be a twin. Maybe you just better let me see that book," and the boy was never sure it was a joke. He would open the book on the bar and the man would study it, frowning. "I don't know, now," he'd say. "Seems that fella last light had a newer book." The boy would grin broadly, keeping fear trapped behind his teeth, always desperately afraid there had been a mistake, a customer given the wrong receipt.

The man in the plaid shirt would say loudly, "Vic, wasn't there a fella just like this one in here last night?"

One of the two or three men bent over the bar would say, "Sure as hell was, Fritz. Looked just like this one. You better call over to the jail, tell Jess to get over here."

For an infinite moment, each time, the boy would wait, para-
lyzed, and then the man in the plaid shirt would bang the book
closed and say, "Nooo, come to think of it, the other one wasn't as
big as this fella here," and the boy's relief would empty his lungs.
He always stood straighter and the man in the plaid shirt would
smack the cash register with a heavy finger, count out two dimes and
a nickel on the bar. In Green's or Durban's, waxed linoleum on the
floor, high chrome-legged stools in front of the bar, padding on the
chairs around the tables, a juke-box's steaming colors in one corner,
there were never any questions but it was uncomfortable in a different way because the man behind the bar never smiled, never really
saw him, simply asked how much and paid.

In Bardulli's the man always wore a sweater, no matter how hot it
was, and his hands were so fragile his spotted skin seemed wrapped
around chicken bones; in the Kozy Korner the man always smoked a
twisted black cigar no bigger than a cigarette; in Sivet's the man
always put the change on the bar with fingers dyed dark brown at
the tips, but they always asked if he was sure he hadn't collected
before and they always said something like, "Two bit's a lot for a
newspaper that don't tell me nothing I can't hear on the radio."
And the boy always agreed it was a lot of money, but that was how
much he had to ask for.

And sometimes—not every Saturday morning, but often—she
would be there, sitting at one of the tables. Never at the bar. Then,
layering his fear, would be something else, a nibbling of tiny cold
teeth inside his chest under the nipples, a deep empty tingling sensation like waking up before it was light and knowing it was an hour
until breakfast.

She was always smiling. But it wasn't a happy smile, not as if
she'd just heard something funny or was thinking of something
pleasant; it was a smile that didn't have any reason behind it and
wasn't going anywhere.

The boy thought she was ugly. Not the definite-reason ugly of
Lucas's huge greyish-brown pitted nose and some kind of growth on
his neck that filled up the space between his ear and shirt collar, so
big you had to swallow hard just seeing it.

Her ugliness fascinated him; he couldn't separate it from the winks or tight-mouthed expressions on people when her name was mentioned. Her ugliness was a bland, total impression spreading out from the smile, taking in her eyes, wet and flatly lustrous like ripe olives under the queer, folded-at-the-corners eyelids, skin shiny with a kind of slippery shine, black hair parted straight up the middle and pulled down on both sides. Her hair looked as if it had been chopped off at the ends. It didn't even look like real hair, not a lot of individual strands, but two solid minutely grooved pieces of polished wood stuck on both sides of her head.

Years later, remembering those Saturday mornings, he would see her in a single garment, a beltless dress, sleeveless, of some dark colorless color and yet he would also remember there was always a single not-white thin strap of a bra or slip on her meaty shoulder where the dress was tugged down. That pale suggestive band on her flesh sent a worm of unfocused desire crawling through his stomach. And, remembering, the Saturday mornings would always be in summer with flies beading long, amber, sticky curls of paper and the fans hung from the high ceilings moved slowly like propellers.

The man in the plaid shirt or the man with the cigar or sweater would say, "Hey now, with all that money you got, maybe you'd like to have yourself a good time. You want to give this fella two bits worth of good time, Annie?" And the men at the bar would laugh. But Annie's smile never changed; it was always the same with her upper lip nipped in showing her front teeth, pushing her nose up so lip and nose formed a soft snout. And the worst of it was, Bascomb, sitting beside her, always in bib overalls thick with grime over a stained long-sleeved undershirt, would smile, too. But it wasn't a smile like Annie's. He would look at the boy and his teeth would show like a dog growling.

The boy wouldn't know where to look: if he watched the man in the plaid shirt or the men leaning on the bar they would laugh harder, hunch their shoulders and slap the bar with their palms. And if he looked at Annie he was consumingly afraid she would *do* something, make some gesture that was invitation and threat. And most of all he didn't dare look at Bascomb because of that smile like the beginning of a howl.

Finally, when the laughter wrapped around the boy so tight he couldn't take a breath, the man in the plaid shirt would say, "O.K., sport. You want a beer to cool you off?" and while the men laughed again the boy would stare at the bar, say no sir and take his money. When he went outside his legs would be trembling and he would carry Annie's flat, shiny face and Bascomb's smile with him.

No one bothered with Annie's last name and no one ever said she was simple-minded. Her name didn't matter, everyone knew who you meant when you said "Annie" and it wasn't necessary to say she was simple-minded, you could tell that just by looking at her. The boy knew her name was Bascomb because it was in his collection book. At least her husband's name was in the book: Lovell Bascomb. But there were smirky whispers that he wasn't her husband at all. That possibility filled the boy with nameless hunger.

Bascomb didn't have a regular job, another strange and inexplicably evil fact. He did odd hauling, trash and coal, in a rusting blackish Chevrolet pick-up with one crumpled blue fender and one fender missing and he did some trapping east of town and sometimes he swamped out one of the taverns—the Kozy Korner or Sivet's, one of those, but never the Silver Dollar or Green's or any of the places on Main Street where the bartenders wore black leather bow ties and the glasses were stacked in sparkling pyramids under the mirror behind the bar.

The boy and his friends traded baseball cards and rumors about Bascomb, rumors that he did vague horrible criminal things. It was common knowledge, with no source and no confirmation, that he had been in jail in Missouri or Indiana for slicing up a farmer or beating a dago 'til the dago was almost dead. That "almost" made the beating real, a definite event.

If Bascomb and Annie were in one of the taverns on Saturday morning he was both sorry and relieved. At least he wouldn't have to collect from Bascomb until evening when he made his deliveries. He dreaded going to Bascomb's with his pocket full of dimes and nickels.

Bascomb's place was on a crooked little half street that cut off to the west midway between Saloon Alley and the Adler House, an erratic unnamed lane of graveled tar ending in muddy indecision in a patch of weedy prairie. The street had only two or three houses, unevenly spaced under tall walnut trees. Bascomb's was cocked at the end of the street; when the boy made his deliveries in the late afternoon the sun was moving down on it. Years later, remembering, he would think here, too, it was perpetual summer, late summer, the humped, shadowed street dotted with dull green walnut hulls and the sun always floated down toward Bascomb's shack—not a house at all, just a squat box of wooden planks chinked with concrete, earth-floored, roofed with corrugated tin weathered brown. As he approached, the angle of the house let the sun touch one window, turning it into a square of orange ice as though the house were on fire inside. And that seemed strange because, even with the fiery window, on the hottest afternoons the shack looked damp and cold.

Summers later, lying beside the slim violin shape of the black-haired woman he married, he would slide into sleep seeing the dark shack frozen in a halo of sun.

And, in those distant summers, lying beside his wife, feeling her heat through the thin sheet, he would watch himself move up to the door of Bascomb's shack and he did not know if he watched from a dream or the last instant of memory before sleep.

Did she really invite him in when he knocked? He would—almost— convince himself, then and later, that he heard her queer drawl, "r's" in unlikely places because of the deformed lip.

He had never been inside before, had only stood on the section of railroad tie that was both step and porch. The interior was cramped and disappointingly tidy, disappointingly average: flour sack curtains on the screenless windows, a table, chipped and slightly canted, flanked by two mismatched chairs, a thick vegetably smell like wet grass. An unfinished wall separated the kitchen and the bedroom.

Those details he would remember later, additions to the memory of the woman. The dress pulled down from her shoulders, falling limp from her wide hips, she stood by the sink, washing. He would remember the exact outline of the pump, a glazed blue and white metal cup hanging from a wire around the pump, a small bottle on the window sill with a few reedy bloomless stalks poking up. A soft voice, not humming exactly, not singing, simply a soft cooing sound from her throat. She was washing with a piece of rough cloth, one thick white arm raised, the fingers loosely curled.

She didn't move when she saw him. He stared and her smile seeped away, returned at once. She lowered her arm, made no move to pull the dress up. Her breasts were heavy waxed gourds pushing brown shadows against her ribs. He was amazed at their color. Not cool white; her flesh above the burnt-clay circles was webbed with pale bluish veins.

She unhooked the cup from the pump. "Warreh?"

Everything she did seemed to be done so slowly. Later, he would wonder about that, would wonder if it had seemed to be so slow then or whether it was a trick of memory. Her plump shoulders quivered as she worked the pump handle.

From far away he heard the slam of Bascomb's truck door. His feet would not move, he could not turn away from the movement of her back, the squeak-gurgle of the pump, the weighted swing of her breast visible between arm and body, her smile over the curve of her shoulder as if she were going to bite herself.

He turned and thudded into Bascomb in the doorway, felt Bascomb's hands heavy on his shoulders, thumbs just brushing his neck, was aware of Bascomb's smell. Bascomb was not smiling, was not looking at him at all.

He stared up into the beard-flecked folds of skin under Bascomb's chin. "I came to collect. She told me to come in!" The voice was someone else's, came from somewhere inside him.

And everything happened so slowly. Bascomb, smiling now, bent over, took an eternity doing it. "You get paid?"

"No."

He struggled with the book, tore off the receipt with fingers that danced uncontrollably. Bascomb took the receipt, slowly so slowly rolled it into a ball between thumb and forefinger. Bascomb said, "I ain't got no money now. You come back later."

He knew it was a test, knew even as he realized it that he would fail, that he would never ask for the money, because that would say he wasn't guilty of anything and he could never do that.

"That's all right? You come back?" Bascomb's voice was lovely, deep and smooth as dark cold water.

He nodded, felt Bascomb's hands loosen, bolted past and through the door.

Later, he would think he could remember the sound of what might have been a soft wet blow, a sound like something dropped from a great height into mud and what might have been a squeal, high, mewling, sweeping up to die in a thin silvery echo. But those sounds were threaded through the crackle of his pounding feet on the road. He ran until he reached Bridget Street and then, breathless, unable to stop, ran faster than he ever would run again until he saw his house.

He never collected from Bascomb again, not for the receipt crushed into a little ball or for any of the weeks after. Each Saturday he tore out Bascomb's receipt and threw it away, rolling it into a little ball first. And Bascomb never offered to pay. Sometimes Bascomb would be sitting on the railroad tie step when he brought the paper and Bascomb would smile and hold out his hand, slowly moving his fingers. The boy always stopped a few feet away and tossed the paper gently, turning to go before Bascomb caught it.

A few years later the shack burned down. Someone said Bascomb and Annie went to Kentucky, but no one knew for sure.

Years later his son applied for a route. The first evening the boy delivered without the supervisor, he followed the boy's bicycle in his car. That night his wife grunted a sleepy rejection when he caressed her hip, but he dug at her secret folds with insistent fingers until she rolled toward him. Later, he lay awake until the bedroom window was smeared with soft grey light.

The Trunk

Andulescu's heart attack sent a tremor along Wilson Avenue, the after-shock vibrating a block on either side. "You hear about Andy? Heart attack. They tooken him over to Weiss Memorial." It was a natural disaster and something terribly unnatural:

D'ja heah— ?

Lake Michigan dried up

The Hancock blew away

Royko's running for the city council

Veeck traded Harry to the Cubs for Brickhouse even up

Andy had a heart attack . . .

Or at least that was the way Flynn viewed it. Flynn heard about it from Rigelli. It had to be a joke except Rigelli had no sense of humor. "Over to Broadway. He just keeled over. Thursday night, late. You been up in Milwaukee or you woulda heard."

Flynn didn't question Rigelli's information, just as he didn't acknowledge he'd been in Milwaukee. Rigelli's news was always hard as concrete, his facts indisputable.

He blinked in the late May sunshine. It was a gorgeous morning, the sky enameled bright blue with a few clouds, plump and heavy as dumplings, sliding toward the lake.

Andulescu in the hospital. The day should be purple-black, streaked with lightning. Dogs should be howling. He was suddenly aware of gaps in the day, missed the familiar bellow, the wave of the perpetually bare hairy arm. The street was normal, crowded, depressingly empty.

Amazing. Even the hospital was unaware of what was happening inside it. People moved around as though nothing had changed in the world. At the desk the grimly pleasant woman automatically raised barricades, but twenty years of skip-tracing and ten as a precinct captain had trained Flynn to deal with such nonsense. Fifteen minutes after he entered he was talking to a pale young man in a white tunic with a breast pocket studded with pencils and gadgets.

Flynn was implacably patient. One by one " . . . not a relative . . . ," " . . . must check with Dr. Stein before allowing . . . " and "absolutely no visitors at this time . . . " were quietly crushed.

He punched 4 in the elevator and rocked on his heels. An old lady in a bathrobe glared suspiciously, sucking in her cheeks. A few gray hairs, stiff as tungsten wire, curled over her pink skull. She smelled old. Flynn smiled. She pulled the bathrobe tight across her chest, wedged her buttocks protectively in the corners. Flynn sighed. Andulescu would have winked at her, made some outrageous proposal to lift her skimpy eyebrows and the corners of her mouth.

Flynn hated hospitals. He always felt someone was going to pop out of a door behind him and wax away his footprints. Most of all he hated the chrome carts. Everything was shoved around: medicine, food, old men with eyes closed and mouths open or lips clamped so tightly the shape of gums was outlined and eyes wide open in silent panic watching the ceiling rush past. Not even little kids cried when they were put on carts.

The door of 403 was half open. That was a good sign. If it was closed they were doing something serious, because if it was only humiliating they didn't care who watched. And if it was wide open there would be a black woman with white stockings bagging at the knees efficiently turning the mattress into a flat, eloquent "c." Flynn felt his thigh twinge. He'd had enough of hospitals.

Andulescu was lying very still, his hair a splatter of inky mop strands on the pillow.

Flynn took a deep breath. "So, here you are."

It was a stupid thing to say, but he couldn't put his head on the immense chest, couldn't say, "Hey, get up, let's talk. Put your arm around me again, hug me til I can't breathe, kiss me on the cheek and laugh so loud when I flinch with embarrassment people shake their heads." If it was Flynn in bed, Andulescu might say something crazy like that, but Flynn could only say, "So, here you are."

"Ay, you English crook, you, what you doing here?" Flynn let his breath out and grinned. Andulescu's careless geography lumped anyone not obviously Balkan into a composite "English." With Flynn, it had become a title.

"I heard you was up here taking a rest."

"So where's the flowers, candy, a big basket fruit?" Andulescu's voice boomed through the door, bounced off the tiled walls. "You visit a sick man, you should bring things! A bottle wine! You bring that?"

Flynn couldn't stop grinning. He'd feared something silent, pale, shrunken, punctured with tubes snaking down from inverted plastic flasks. He pulled a chair close to the bed and sat down. This was the old Andulescu and—no, sitting close, he could see it wasn't. There were bruise-tinted smudges on the eyelids, the skin had a gray undertone, the jowls were looser. He wrapped his fingers together and rested his hands in his lap to keep from patting the arm on the sheet.

"Next time I'll bring a bottle."

"Next time! No next time! Tomorrow, the next day for sure, they throw me out!"

A nurse squeaked in on the echo of Andulescu's roar. Flynn let himself be ushered out.

"Hey, you come back here, you bring one of Rigelli's pizzas!"

Flynn flipped a wave from the door. "I'll do that. You take it easy."

Grinning, he followed the nurse, watched her stiffen at, "Lots of mushrooms!"

The nurse stalked into the glass-walled island midway down the hall. Flynn was surprised she didn't go back to 403 to quiet Andulescu. He leaned his elbows on the counter and waited for her to notice him. He asked her what exactly was Andulescu's condition and nodded solemnly through the automatic rebuff.

He never questioned his gift, knew only that for some reason—a demand for confidences in the receptive moon of his face, something blandly paternal or at least avuncular in his eyes—he eventually had his questions answered. It was a small, invaluable gift. The secret was to lean patiently against refusal until you got what you wanted. And, of course, never be too ambitious in your wanting. Finally: no, Mr. Andulescu (she pronounced it properly, softening the final syllable; Flynn could hear the thunderous correction rocketing down the hall) was in no *immediate* danger *but* of course a man his age, one must *always* be concerned in cases like this. He let the litany of medical jargon drift through him. A heart attack, then? Well, no, not really a heart attack that was not a precise term but yes it might be *called* that. Mild, a warning . . . would have to avoid . . . be careful of strenuous . . . the doctor would prescribe . . .

Flynn thanked her courteously and started away, then turned back. Had Mr. Andulescu's son been notified? A shuffling of papers, a frown. Why no, the forms had been properly filled out, but there was nothing here about Mr. Andulescu specifying anyone to notify. Flynn nodded again. Not even me, he thought.

A chill wind nipped at him when he went outside. A thick layer of rumpled velour covered the blue. He coaxed the Ford through traffic, worrying about the transmission and thinking about Andulescu.

His office felt damp. Flynn eased his chair back, propped his feet on the windowsill, plucked at the memory of a crease in his trouser leg while information searched for the number. How many Andulescus could there be in Royal Oak, Michigan?

Andulescu's son, Paul, accepted the news sensibly, asked how serious it was, said he would catch the first available flight out of Detroit. Flynn heard him telling someone else his father had had a heart attack. Flynn offered to meet him at O'Hare, was mildly disappointed when the offer wasn't refused. He hung up, sighed, and called the airport.

Flynn enjoyed the ride. The Ford deserved a rest so he took a cab. The sky had changed again, now was flat slate streaked with salmon and lemon swirls. The cabbie made a quick, furtive appraisal of Flynn's guileless face and took him on an extended tour of the western suburbs. Flynn admired the neat homes, the streets where trees formed thick interlocked arches and spattered the hood with irregular dots of lights, was relaxed by the miles of sprinklers flipping irridescent rainbows over lush lawns.

He had never approached O'Hare from the west and was a little sorry when the ride ended. He nodded pleasantly at the astronomical meter number, showed the cabbie one of the many badges he'd accumulated over the years and suggested they discuss the novel route with the stolid cop patting his stomach in front of Continental's terminal. The cabbie wondered why he had considered Flynn so gullible and spat expertly, missing Flynn's shoe by an inch. They decided that six dollars was a fair price. Flynn said the drive was so nice the cabbie must have enjoyed it, too, and that pleasure was worth more than any tip he could give.

Sitting on plastic chairs in the waiting area, Flynn and Andulescu's son drank coffee out of paper cups. Flynn saw similarities: Paul had his father's immensely knuckled hands, the weightlifter's neck, the same coarsely-boned ridge over dark eyes. But the voices were different. And Andulescu's explosion of thick black hair, the almost simian torso—Paul was stocky only, merely darkhaired. The son lacked his father's exuberance. He seemed somehow older than Andulescu. But Flynn liked the boy. I'm getting old, he thought. Paul was not a boy. Mid-forties, at least.

The brief initial unease dissolved quickly. Paul swirled his cup, watching the light move in fractured patterns on the surface. "You know, I tried to get him to come and live with us. We've got enough room, but—well, you know how he is."

Flynn knew. He couldn't imagine Andulescu, coatless, sleeves pushed back over cudgel-shaped arms, rampaging through Royal Oak. No, he could picture it, had a flashing vision of Andulescu, thick bowed legs stamping, hair a wet mane, laughing through miles of lawn sprinklers while an anguished chorus of Pauls brandished rakes and pruning shears in pursuit.

"You know—funny what you think about, the things you remember—he still sends me ten dollars on my birthday? In cash. I can almost tell you how he's doing by what he sends. A brand-new ten, two fives, ten crumpled ones with scotch tape . . . " Paul shook his head, a gesture of exasperated wonder. "And he always sends flowers on my mother's birthday. Every year—never a Christmas card, nothing like that—but every year for her birthday. And every year it comes a week early. Somehow, he's got it in his head it's May 10th. A couple of times, I told him, but . . . it's hard to surprise her, you know? I mean, with a card coming like that, a week early. I tried to tell him, but . . . "

"What's your stepfather think about that?" Flynn wasn't curious, it was only conversation. It couldn't matter now, after all this time. He couldn't even remember why he knew there was a stepfather.

"Nothing. You mean, does it still bother him? No, Jack's all right." Flynn couldn't detect any undertones. Maybe there was something revealing in the voice so neutral. That didn't matter now, either. He did wonder if there was a lingering resentment over Andulescu's abandonment of his wife and son. If there was, he couldn't hear it. It was either buried too deeply or had been worn away long ago.

"Well, I wasn't sure. About calling you, I mean. Andy talked about you, your kids, stuff like that, but I didn't know . . ." He shrugged. What else was there to say? The Ford was going to need major repairs, that was certain. He should have minded his own business.

"No, really, I'm glad you did." The cup moved from side to side. "I don't know what to do about him. I really don't. I don't know what I'm *supposed* to do. I can't drag him home with me. I thought maybe a retirement home, but—can you imagine him in some place like that?" No, that Flynn couldn't imagine. "We—Karen, my wife—" Flynn had seen her in a snapshot Andulescu had, a nice looking lady, neat, with maybe just a touch too much jaw. "We thought maybe we could talk him into going down to Florida. Jack's brother's down there. Been there for a couple of years. He likes it."

"It's an idea," Flynn said. Andulescu in Florida, dozing in the sun? With all-right-Jack's brother?

"He's got a pretty good pension, some social security. We could pad it out. He'd have enough."

You're talking like he's some kind of old man, Flynn thought. I'm old, this Jack's brother, he sounds old, *you're* old already. An-

dulescu is—he's Andulescu. He doesn't even know what old means.
What would this Jack's brother do when Andulescu came whooping
in in the middle of the night, slammed a jug on the table, ate raw
onions like they were apples, started to sing the funny songs that
sounded like laughter and weeping at the same time?

What would Flynn do when Andulescu wasn't around to do those
things?

What would it be like without Andy to offer him an onion,
without an Andulescu to sit across from him at two in the morning,
tipping a wine bottle with his throat working like a piston and then,
wiping his mouth with that black-napped forearm, yelling, "Noroc!
Mult noroc, you English crook you! I love you!"

"You want to stay at Andy's place? I can get you in."

"No, I called ahead for a reservation over at the Sheraton.
Thanks anyway."

They walked through the terminal. Paul moved heavily, each step
a careful advance. His father always moved at a near-trot, chest out
as though he was pushing his way through walls.

"He's a funny guy."

Flynn nodded. "Sometimes he is."

"No, I mean it. One time—he was in Philadelphia then. I guess
that was just before he came here. I went to see him between semes-
ters. I hadn't seen him for—god, I don't know. Since I was little. I
just decided to see him. He was living in this little one-room place
and he had a dog. I didn't know what to say to him after I got there.
I mean, he hugged me and pounded me on the back and I didn't
know what to say. So—through here?—so I said, what's the dog's
name? And he said, how the hell do I know? I don't talk dog! And
he laughed. My god, when he laughed . . . a funny guy."

Flynn didn't know how to respond to that. "He doesn't have a
dog now."

They went out into the cool evening.

Flynn could see changes in Andulescu, small, subtle alterations,
movements fractionally less brisk, just a shade less volume in the
voice.

"So you're going to Florida."

"Sure, all us ritzy-bitzy guys go to Florida. That's where you should go. Do you good. Fix up your blood."

"What about your stuff?"

"Leave it here, what you think? You think I'm going away for always? Go see this Charley What's-his-name, swim in the ocean, catch some fish, watch the pretty college girls. Then I'm come back here."

"Rigelli going to keep your room?"

"He rents it, I come back here and kick hell out whoever it is. And Rigelli, too. Naaah, this is my place. You keep a good eye on this, eh?"

"This": a few magazines, two concave-sided cardboard boxes stuffed with tools and odd bits of clothing, a lurid print of the Sacred Heart in a gilt frame, an assortment of clocks that Andulescu repaired and then gave away, the old trunk with its domed lid and leather handles.

"So, how you feeling?"

"Great!" The meaty wedge of hand thumped his chest. Was there a little less force? A wince? "Listen you, my old man, he lived to one hundred and twenty years old with all his teeth and hair and I got more health than him."

"Last time you said a hundred ten."

"I just remember a couple more years. Don't let nothing happen to my trunk, eh? My great-great-gran'father, he got that from his father."

"Bullshit."

The grin huge. "Maybe. Just a little bit."

Flynn received no postcards with artificially blue water and palm trees silhouetted against an impossible sky, but he wasn't disappointed. Well, just a little bit. The street was the same, the constant thrum of music from the hillbilly bars went on, but for Flynn there was a difference.

The night Paul had arrived, outside the terminal, after they formally shook hands, Paul had said, "Well, I'm glad you called me, Mr. Flynn. I'll go over and see him first thing in the morning. He's lucky to have a friend like you."

Flynn had shrugged. The shrug was habitual, a form of punctuation. "He'd do the same for me."

It was something to say. But it wasn't true. There would have been no one of Flynn's for Andulescu to call. And Andulescu wouldn't have done the same thing, even if there was someone interested enough to take a plane from Michigan to see Flynn in the hospital. Andulescu would have said, "Flynn? Flynn? Naaah! Him and me, we were drinking the wine just last night, right here!" And he would have roared that Flynn, that English crook, was a good man, a beautiful man. He would have wept, copiously, sincerely. He would have said he loved Flynn, meaning it. And he would have drunk a Rumanian toast.

But he wouldn't have called anyone, wouldn't have remembered if there was someone to call. That was all right. For Flynn, Andulescu was enough just being Andulescu: a rumbling laugh among tight smiles, an encircling arm in a world of moist, tentative handshakes, a klaxon greeting from a block away.

Flynn had called Michigan, his finger idly tracing graffitti scratched in the second-hand desk top while he talked to Andulescu's son. The conversation quiet, unemotional. Andulescu would have been positive, immediate, a roar of the moment. Different people, Flynn knew. Still, a postcard, just a little note running a thread into Andulescu's world, would have been nice.

Flynn had called Michigan; and, if he had been there when Andulescu collapsed, he would have efficiently summoned aid, might even have pressured the chest and given mouth-to-mouth in the proper way. But if Flynn had collapsed, Andulescu would have scooped him up, would have carried him blocks to the hospital, brushing aside all interference. Inefficient? Of course. Probably fatal? Again, of course. But Flynn wasn't sure his was the better way.

For a while Rigelli asked, "You hear anything from Andy?"

"No, you know him."

After a week Rigelli stopped asking, but he didn't rent Andulescu's room.

"Ay! You English crook you! What's matter, you don't see your old friends!"

Flynn waited for a break in the traffic, but before he could cross Andulescu was dancing across the street, throwing his arms wide, impervious to the screech of tires, the obscenities.

"So, you came back." Flynn felt his ribs bend dangerously.

"Sure I come back! Didn't I tell you?"

Flynn was conscious of people frowning, stepping around them. He rubbed his cheek. "You're a sloppy kisser."

"What you know about kissing, eh? Pit-pit-pit! Like a little girl with her gran'ma. Cristosu Dummeseu! Tell you what. I let you buy me some wine!"

"It's too early."

"Naaah! Never too early for wine. Only too late. C'mon, you!"

They moved into the Deluxe, Flynn wrapped in a furry arm. Andulescu bellowed a greeting, reached across the bar to shake Morrie's shoulders. Flynn eased onto a stool. Andulescu didn't look good at all. Beneath the chest the belly was gaunt, the old drum-tight swell shrunken. There was a yellowish discoloration in the eyes, a splintered pattern of red veins. The cheek-flesh looked spongy under the tan.

"You don't look so good."

"I look great!" The sturdy column of throat had softened. Flynn tried not to watch Andulescu's Adam's apple slide under the slack skin. There were ropy cords beneath the chin.

"You been sick?"

Andulescu scrubbed his scalp with both hands. "Me? Sick? Listen, my old man, he was one hundred and maybe twenty years and—naaah. Ah, something with the kidneys, a little bit in the chest. Nothing."

"So, how was Florida?"

Andulescu banged his glass, squeezed Morrie's arm when he came with the bottle. "Oh, that's some place! Terrible! You wouldn't believe. Old people. Miles and miles, nothing but old people!" An exaggerated shudder. "Listen, they got this street—what they call Collins Avenue? By the ocean?—people are sitting on porches.

They got these hotels with porches. You know what they're doing all day? Nothing! All day! At night they go inside, sit and watch television! I say, let's go down, swim in the ocean, catch some fish, watch pretty girls. They look like I'm crazy! This Charley—a nice guy, very clean, but—in his bathroom, it's like a drugstore! Big bottles, little bottles, green pills, white pills, two-color pills. Take a pill before you eat, take two pills after you eat, take this pill to poop, take this pink stuff to stop pooping . . . !"

Flynn watched their reflection in the mirror. "Well, I'm glad you're back." He didn't feel glad. This wasn't the old Andulescu. Maybe just getting used to not having Andulescu around, having the memory not the man, had something to do with it.

In November Andulescu was back in the hospital. Flynn visited twice. He didn't call Michigan this time. He knew it wasn't fatal, was—this time—just the first in an inevitable series. He didn't know how he knew.

The second time he went to the hospital he took a bottle of wine and Andulescu told him about the old man in St. Petersburg. He had saved the clipping, one of the two-paragraph fillers that was newsworthy only because of its catalog of afflictions—phlebitis, angina, fourteen operations—and the suicide's method—dousing himself with gasoline and setting himself afire—made the death of another old man an item in the paper, a death not tragic nor even sad, only bizarre, something for the Guinness book: the oldest varidiseased man in Florida to incinerate himself.

"What are you holding on to junk like that for?"

"I don't know. Is that something? To make a show like that? What's the sense? People just laugh for you."

"That's what I mean, it's junk." The windows were tinted so that, outside, the day, the season, never changed, merely shifted, brightening, darkening, between shades of sepia. The snow didn't look real, a dusting of cocoa on the parking lot.

Flynn wondered if he was catching cold. His appetite was gone and cigarettes tasted like hot ashes. He rubbed a bare patch in the steamed window and watched Andulescu move the bricks inside.

After ten trips half the bricks remained on the sidewalk. The old Andulescu would have dashed up the stairs three at a time, finishing the job in ten minutes. Fifteen at the outside.

Andulescu was wearing a frayed, once-white wool sweater. Flynn had never seen him with his arms covered.

He went downstairs, banged the swollen door open and stepped outside, shivering. "You want some help?"

"I need help from a skinny crook like you, eh?" The voice didn't boom, came out flat, edgeless.

"You building something?"

"No. Something, yeah."

"You want to go over by Morrie's?"

Cars crept tentatively over the slippery river of slush between them.

"No, O.K., sure, maybe later."

Flynn sat with his chin propped in his palm. He sipped beer and rolled poker dice with Morrie for an hour. He broke even playing liar's poker with Benny Quick. Andulescu didn't show up.

Flynn debated navigating the Ford through the icy streets, shrugged, walked the four blocks to his apartment, legs awkwardly spraddled to keep his balance. It was snowing again when he turned off the light.

Rigelli didn't call Flynn. Flynn saw the ambulance from his window. He didn't hurry. His nose itched. Definitely a cold. The Spanish-looking attendant was closing the rear doors when he crossed the street.

Rigelli moved his hands vaguely, then tucked them back under his apron. "Prob'ly sometime last night. He was still dressed so it was prob'ly early."

"Heart?"

"That's what the guy there says. Prob'ly was. He was havin' trouble with it."

"Can I go up? He had some of my stuff up there."

Rigelli shrugged. "Sure, why not."

Flynn tried to push the trunk with his toe. It wouldn't move. He sat on the bed and rubbed his knees. He closed his eyes. He saw Andulescu, face sweat-lacquered, grinning hugely, straining at the trunk, listening for the pop or snap or whatever it was inside his chest.

He went outside and tip-toed across the street to call Michigan. He'd go back later and empty the trunk, put the bricks someplace. Maybe he could use them in the Ford trunk as long as the streets were slippery.

The Milk-glass Chicken

Hobie could judge what kind of day it was likely to be when the bus turned at Dorsett and sat, rumbling, while Suspenders painfully crabbed his way up the high steps. The old man always wore grey wash pants a mile too big for him and wide pale-green suspenders that hiked the pants up high on his chest. While Suspenders inched his way up the fat chrome railing and stood, breathing heavy, pulled over like a cooked shrimp by the suspenders, poking change around in his palm with a shaky finger—he never had the right change sorted out, always had six or seven dimes and quarters to finger through—Hobie could look down at the parking lot behind Main and see if Fish Ear's car was in its parking place.

If Fish Ear's place was empty, it could be raining hard enough to strangle a frog and Hobie would smile and nod. Easy day coming up. But if Fish Ear's car was there, no matter how sunny it might be, Hobie knew he was in for some kind of hassle. One good thing about Fish Ear was his predictableness. Give him that, if he was coming to work he never snuck up on you. Always got there at 7:00, a full half hour before he had to, and then he'd sit in the cafeteria getting in kitchen staff's way, hunched over a table drinking black coffee and thinking up miseries for everybody.

Actually, there were two good things about Fish Ear, the other being his rheumatism or arthritis or whatever it was scrunching him up. More and more lately he couldn't make it in to work and so every day Hobie would look down into the parking lot.

Hobie took his time. He could see if Fish Ear was there as soon as the bus turned the corner, but he avoided looking until he heard the clink of Suspenders' fare in the box. It took will power to hold off like that. Come on, old man, get on with it. One of these days he was going to stay on the bus, just to see where Suspenders went every day.

He lit the morning's third cigarette, heard the coins drop. Damn, there sat the old shiny Ford, a cream and scarlet threat to Hobie's day. Why would a man buy an ugly car like that?

He put his lunch sack in his locker and changed into the crisp white pants, jacket and shoes, slammed the door and slapped it with his palm to make sure the lock caught. Should he go on up to 1A and let Fish Ear try to find him or go down to the cafeteria and get it out of the way? Some days it was amusing to drift through Main, sticking his head in Accounting to sugar up Watkins, popping in on Squints to nibble the cookies she always had, officiously moving a table from one alcove to another and always staying just a calculated and tantalizing few steps ahead of Fish Ear. He'd let Fish Ear catch a glimpse of him and it was all he could do to keep from laughing out loud at old Fish Ear, stomping and wheezing and muttering, always just around a corner or coming in one door while Hobie was sliding out another. There were days Hobie could dawdle away thirty, forty-five minutes before he let Fish Ear catch up with him.

He stretched lazily and admired his reflection in the mirror, adjusted his jacket so it hung just so. Making Fish Ear chase him today was too much trouble.

"Williams."

Hobie glided past the cafeteria door, pretending not to hear. He moved very slowly, but somehow gave the impression of determined progress. He always moved at the same leisurely pace but, with a curious lift of his shoulders or swing of his arms or a change in the slap of his white shoes on the waxed tiles, he could adjust the appearance of his speed.

"Williams!"

Hobie stopped, brow furrowed, obviously puzzled, obviously trying to find the voice's source. He turned and smiled broadly at Fish Ear's limping approach.

"Hey, good morning, Mr. Froehman. That you callin' me? Hey, you lookin' goooood today." Sometimes Winnie told him he was going to get himself in real trouble someday, making himself out the fool like that, larding his voice with minstrel Delta. He didn't think so. Hell, Froehman *expected* it; it never dawned on Fish Ear that Hobie had lived his whole life more than a mile farther north, up on Hister, or that Hobie's junior college credits counted for more than Fish Ear's dropping out of high school.

Fish Ear never looked him square in the face. "Gamow's on vacation this week and Upton called in sick again." It was a wonder, the way Fish Ear could say "drunk" with brittle disgust and make it come out "sick." And it was a constant wonder how the man could hear anything with those squinchy, pulled-in ears like a fish's gills.

"Aw, nawh. Hey, I'm sorry to hear that. Poor old Upton sick again? He just don't take proper care of himself at all, that man, I saw him just last night . . . "

Fish Ear's eyes flicked Hobie's chin. "Doing what?"

"As I remember . . . " Hobie pretended to concentrate. Fish Ear thought they all knew each other, all sat around sipping warm wine every night, all lived in a sharply defined circle. How did a man *survive* being so stupid? "He was down by the Seven Spot Lounge . . . "

"Drinking?"

Sometimes Hobie was almost bored with the game. "Aw, nawh, Mr. Froehman." Someday he was going to slip and say "Fish Ear."

"Upton? Nawh, he's a deacon. Down by the Seven Spot, that's just where I *saw* him. He just come out of the drug store with this stuff for his throat. I could see he was feelin' poorly . . . "

Fish Ear's eyes slid up toward Hobie's, came as high as his cheekbones. "Yeh, sure. O.K., you go over to C today and help out Harris."

Damn, wouldn't you just know? Pick the one building that's a perfect bitch and you'd pick C every time.

He made a leisurely detour through 1A, pausing to share a few cookies with Squints. It was a wonder her eyes just didn't pop right out, the way her forehead pushed down on them. But she was generally friendly.

Originally, the job with the Dumont Home for the Aged was going to be a very temporary thing, something to put food on the table
until he found something better. Winona had agreed he wasn't cut
out to spend his life pushing a mop around after a bunch of droolly
old folks. Occasionally he still mentioned doing something else
someday, but they both knew it was too late. Not that it mattered all
that much. A job was a job. The pay wasn't all that good, not what
he could make over to Ford as an assembler, but it wasn't all that
bad either. And the work wasn't all that hard once you learned what
to watch out for and didn't do something stupid like trying to wres-
tle down some spooky old man all by yourself instead of going by
the rules and calling for assistance.

Learn the rules backwards and forwards, that was something he
caught on to easy. Just like the army. You didn't have to follow all
of them, that was silly. But when trouble came up, if you knew the
rules and selected the right one you'd come out O.K. Of course not
all the rules together would stop you from getting a rap in the head
now and then, but you were pretty stupid if you let it get to be a
habit.

And no rule would save you from a lap full of vomit now and then
because it seemed like some days every one of them was just saving
up a stomach full of goop to dump on you. But you could even turn
something disgusting like that into a bonus, taking your time cleaning up, making one trip down to the laundry to get rid of the messed-
up jacket and pants and then fooling around here and there before
making another trip over to stores to draw clean stuff. Just as long
as you looked like the whole thing was necessary. Even if you're
standing still, you got to learn to make it look like you're doing it for
a reason and you'll be all right.

The most important thing was to take a sensible approach to the
whole thing and not get to feeling sorry for this one or getting a mad
on about that one because none of them were going to outlast you.
Just pick the job up at the front gate like a sack, carry it around with
you—and make sure nobody stuck a lot of heavy stuff in there on
you—and drop it at the gate on the way out.

He blinked in the bright sunlight and lit a cigarette before ambling
over to C. On the sparse lawn two slumped figures, wrapped in

blankets in spite of the warmth, dozed in wheelchairs. Behind them
a lean orderly stood in the shade of a maple. The orderly waved and
Hobie lifted a limp hand in return.

"How's Winona?"

"Gettin' better," Hobie yelled. "Summer cold, that's all."

That was another bonus working here. You could get medicine
for nothing. Just tell Humpty-Dumpty the symptoms and he'd send
you over to get a few pills of this or a bottle of that—five or six
dollars saved every time.

"Where you headed?"

Hobie rolled his eyes. "C!"

"Oh, my." The orderly giggled. One of the slumped figures
raised its head. They looked just like turtles when they did that,
sticking their necks out and moving their heads real slow and blinking.

No matter how much it was scrubbed, C had a peculiar smell all
its own, a sour, old-people odor, and he wrinkled his nose. When
they got too bad to keep out in the open or needed special attention
or started acting crazy all the time instead of just once in a while,
they got shoved into C.

He found Harris and a new nurse, a fat one, in the small office on
the second floor. Harris motioned him to a seat and he waited while
the nurse gave her orders for the day and Harris pretended to listen.
Hobie grinned. Harris had been running C the way he wanted to for
almost twenty years, but every time a new nurse showed up, she
tried to change things around according to some book. When she
left, Harris told him to take the third floor and Hobie groaned. On
the third floor you could expect a mess of some kind.

"How many you got up there?"

"Seven."

That wasn't too bad. Two empty rooms. Of course it depended on
what seven they were. Hobie hadn't been on C3 for almost two
months.

"Ol' Faithful still here?"

Harris tilted his chair back, scrubbed his shiny scalp. "Mr. Singer
is still with us."

Mr. Singer was a spitter, the worst spitter Hobie ever saw. A lot of old people, now and then, for no reason whatever, they'd haul off and spit at you, but Old Faithful was something else. Any time you came around—*any* time—you better have an umbrella. You'd swear he was sound asleep, but as soon as you got close his eyelids snapped open like a window shade rolling up and he'd get you right in the face. It was a wonder, the way so much gooey wet came out of such a dried-up little man. And it kept coming, three, four times, as many as he could get off before you got your fingers into his cheeks and pried his mouth open. Even then, the drool ran over your wrist like there was a leaky hose under his tongue.

It was a funny thing about old people. It wasn't only Old Faithful, the difference between a shriveled-up outside and a wet inside. A lot of them, they looked dry as a locust shell stuck on a pear tree, but if they couldn't hold their water or bowels anymore you were always changing and sponging up after them, even if you knew they hadn't drunk a drop or had a bit to eat for a whole day. It was like the outside got old and dry and shoved the wet inside so it stayed juicy.

"You still got the Crusher?" You could put up with the spitters and the biters and all the rest, but that old man frightened Hobie. Seventy years old, he was still so strong the seams threatened to pop on the restraint when he strained. Crazy as anything and strong as a bull; that was a combination to scare anybody. You couldn't keep him in restraint all the time. . . .

Harris blinked. "He died more'n a month ago. You didn't know that?"

"Poor old man," Hobie said, relieved.

"Yeah, ol' sonuvabitch had a stroke. Then there's Mrs. Tazarelli, Mr. Ferguson, Mr. Wodjacysky, Mrs. Mack . . ."

Hobie ticked them off, matching titles and indistinct faces or bodies or traits: Titless Taz, Jaws—Ferguson was a biter, a real snapper—Alphabet Soup, The Truck.

" . . . Washington . . . oh, yeah, and Mrs. Cheney."

"The Chicken Lady? She still here?"

"Oh, yeah. Just the same as always."

How about that? He just assumed she died.

C was an old building, the original old folks home. The concrete block at the front steps and it was built in 1889. Hobie liked it because it was more like a house than a hospital except for the big tubes running down the outside. A lot of wood that had turned almost black with time, creaky old stairs and carved banisters rubbed thin and glossy, high ceilings and tall skinny windows and fancy little plaster decorations in odd places like along the ceiling and over the closets. A rickety old place, but nice.

Automatically he took the stairs because that took longer than riding the elevator. Imagine that, the Chicken Lady. He was on C3 when she came and of course everybody knew all about her even before she showed up because of all the fuss in the newspapers and on the television. He stopped and snapped his fingers; he was so surprised the Chicken Lady was still alive he forgot to ask who was running the third floor.

There were five rooms on the right and four on the left (the fifth had been changed years ago when they put in the elevator). At the far end of the narrow hall a screen-enclosed porch hung out over the south lawn. All the room doors were open and he checked them as he strolled past. It was something you did naturally after a while, not really lookin' in, not really seeing them in there, just passing by. What stopped you was when you *didn't* see them.

The tattered grey cardigan on the porch brightened him. Bitzer never caused problems, just showed up in her tatty old sweater, put in her time and went home. If it wasn't for her white socks and shoes she could be a patient, that's how old she was. Her sturdy shoes, propped on the sagging webbing of an aluminum-framed chair, wagged a greeting. Nothing flapped Bitzer. She was an old-timer, let Harris do what he wanted. She was strong enough to lend a hand, too, and that was a help.

"Hey, how you doin' this fine morning. Cream and double sugar, right?"

She nodded and Hobie went back down to the main floor to the coffee machine, stopping for a leisurely cigarette in the men's room. When he returned to the porch they exchanged desultory gossip and watched the shifting of the wheelchairs on the lawn.

"Time to check," she said, pretending to rise.

"You sit still. You probably pushed enough for two people this morning. I'll look in on 'em."

That was the way you got along. He'd have to check, no matter what, but if she had to order him then she could stick in a lot of piddley junk—check this, wash that, make sure Mr. Ferguson is clean, that kind of stuff. Bitzer was an old-timer and they got along just fine.

He hesitated when he went into the Crusher's room. That was one scary old man. They'd shifted The Truck in there now, a huge snore-whistling lump under the blanket. If they were all like her, wouldn't that be something. Just sleep all day, get shook awake to eat and take the pills, then back to sleep. She was like a big bear, hibernating. Probably messed herself up in her sleep, but he could take care of that later.

"I've got a pain, right here." Whiny voice. The hand poking out of the bathrobe sleeve was nothing but skin and bones, dry thin twigs in a withered glove of mottled brown. A finger scraped a wrinkled cheek. Hobie leaned closer, careful to keep his hands behind him. Dumb old man pulled the same stunt every time. The first time, Hobie made the mistake of touching the skin where the finger was pointing and he thought Jaws was going to chew his thumb off. If you stayed clear of him, he wasn't much trouble.

"Probably got a bad tooth there."

"They're all false." The grin was hideous, those young strong teeth shoving out between the old lips.

"Termites, then," Hobie said, and the old man thought that was very funny.

Titless Taz made him jumpy.

"How you doin' this fine morning?"

Her smile was gentle and vacant. "Just fine, Howard." She didn't remember his name—hell, she didn't remember Bitzer's name. Every time Hobie came close to her the flesh on his chest contracted. She didn't cause trouble either, but one of these days she was going to do something. You could feel it. Took a knife and sliced off her own breast! The damnedest thing. For no good reason, just whacked it right off one day in her own kitchen. All day long she just sat, hugging her arms around her lop-sided chest, kind of rocking back and forth, singing to herself. Quiet, always gave you that soft little-girl smile. . . . One of these days, though . . .

Hobie never tried to pronounce Alphabet Soup's name, just asked him how he was doing this fine morning.

"You got any cigarettes?" A pitiful attempt to be clever. The voice always surprised, clear and echoey like it came from a mile deep from the wreckage of a body like that. The old man had his arms and legs curled up like a dead spider.

"No, sir, now I sure haven't."

"Well," the old man said with bludgeoning slyness, "gimme a match. I got a cigarette around here somewhere."

Hobie patted his pockets vigorously. "I ain't got match one." Just like you made sure there was never any way for Taz to get at anything sharp, you kept matches, lighters, anything that could cause a spark away from Alphabet Soup.

"Would you get me some?" He tried so hard to be nonchalant, but his eyes were huge with pleading.

"I'll go look for some."

"You promise?"

"Oh, sure. I'll see if I can find you some of them big wooden kitchen matches."

"Hurry up."

Hobie didn't think he was teasing the old man. Just the thought of getting his hands on some matches made him happy and he'd forget all about the promise in a few minutes.

Old Faithful was right where he ought to be, sitting in his chair, looking out the window. Hobie stuck his head in the door, keeping well back out of range, and went on.

Washington—Hobie never bothered to think up a name for him—grinned and waved and Hobie grinned back.

"Brother, you're looking fine today."

Washington looked like a banker or some kind of executive, even in his pajamas and bathrobe. Always got up just so, clean and neat and shaved so close his skin was like the caramel on a taffy apple. Got visited regular by his kids, both of them doing all right on their own. You might wonder what Washington was doing in a place like this until he started to talk. The most confusing nonsense you ever heard.

"And you, sir, appear in the best of health."

"Can't complain. How you doin' this fine morning?"

"Splendidly, splendidly." Washington touched the precise elongated vee of mustache. "Did I mention they're here again this morning? Quite a few, you know."

"Is that a fact?"

"Most assuredly."

"Came early, did they?"

Washington's smile was natural, confident. "Quite early. Of course I heard their claws and managed to get the closet open in time."

Hobie made his eyes large, rolled them toward the doorless closet.

"You got them locked up good?"

The laughter was a low tremor. "Oh, your fears are groundless, young man. I can assure you, they present no danger . . ." the smile was beatific "-as-long-as-you SMELL THEM! Do you understand, sir?"

"Oh, I do. That I do."

"Good. Excellent." His beautiful hand clasped Hobie's shoulder, squeezed. He touched the delicate flare of a nostril and winked. *"That's* the secret."

"I'll sure keep that in mind."

Hobie stopped at the door and watched the Chicken Lady. After a while you kind of got used to them and, no matter what they did, no matter how weird it was, they were just repeating something someone did last week, maybe in the same room. Just to keep them sorted out in your own mind you had to give them special names because without that they were just the same old people over and over again.

But the Chicken Lady . . . Hobie shook his head. There still wasn't enough of her to feed a hungry dog. Couldn't weigh no more than seventy-five pounds, if that. Got to give her credit for lasting this long. Way she looked when she came, even after all that time in the hospital, you wouldn't think she'd hang on for a week. She didn't look much better now.

"And how are you this fine mornin'?"

It was like watching a low motion picture, the way her head came up and she looked at him with eyes that filled up almost her whole face like those big-eyed kid pictures at Woolworth's. In her lap, her frail hands spread over it protectively, that same milk-glass chicken she had when they found her. Wasn't nothing in it but some old rusty bobby pins, at least that's what Bitzer said was in there, but if you tried to tug it away from her she wouldn't fight or anything but her hands would just kind of lock. Stronger than the Crusher when it came to holding on to that chicken.

"Hey, you lookin' good." That was a plain lie. Starved down so she was nothing but pinched-up skin. No one ever figured out how long she'd been locked up like that, up in that dirty little room. Treat an old lady like that just so they could cash her measly social security checks. That was really something.

"I want to go home."

That was what made her crazy. You couldn't get her to say anything else, talk about anything, shift her mind on to something else. No matter what you said to her, back she'd come to saying she wanted to go home. Hell, there *wasn't* any home, she ought to know that. House was sold and even when they got out of jail her kid and his wife sure weren't going to hang around. The neighbors would—well, the neighbors would do something. If he lived next door to somebody who did something like that to somebody, let alone his own mother . . .

"Not today. Hey, you want a Pepsi Cola?" She'd hardly touched her breakfast, just a nibble. Even that might be squirreled away in that stupid chicken. You'd think after being locked up like that, with hardly anything at all to eat for all that time, she'd stuff down anything she could get her hands on. The television said when they found her she had a skimpy piece of bread, hard as rock, in that chicken. "You want I should get you a glass of milk?"

She hardly even dented the bed, just rested on the edge like a dandelion fluff.

"Hey, tell you what. If I go down and talk real sweet, I think I can get you a cup of hot chocolate. How about that?"

He didn't know why he bothered.

"No c'mon! I'm not talkin' about some watery junk out of a machine. I mean, real hot chocolate."

"Can I go home?"

He lifted his shoulders, let them slump. "Well, not today. Maybe tomorrow we can talk about it. Here, let me put you in your chair." She didn't resist. It was like lifting an empty box. "There, how's that? Hey, tell you what. How about later on I take you out in the sun for a while?"

Her hands were so thin and drained out you could almost see that stupid chicken through them.

What with one thing and another, the day passed pretty quick and it wasn't too bad, despite finding Fish Ear first thing. Somebody left a *Reader's Digest* lying around and between checks he chuckled at the funny little things they put at the ends of the stories. Bitzer had already read most of them so it was easy to talk about them. Once, he just plain forgot and Old Faithful sprayed him good and made him mad, but except for that the day wasn't bad.

While the doctor was going around, he took his time going back to Main for his lunch sack and was pleased that Winnie put a tomato in with the sandwich.

In the afternoon he dragged a mop over the hall, taking his time, drawing big wet swirls. It wasn't hard and it felt good to move around. Since Bitzer didn't tell him to do it, he didn't have to think up reasons not to.

"You think she's crazy?"

They were on the porch, sipping coffee. It was a wonder how she could drink it like that, sticky with sugar. "Who?"

"The Chicken Lady."

It was something to talk about, to stretch out over a few minutes.

"Well, I think she may be a little senile," Bitzer said. "But what the poor old dear went through, it's no wonder. Anyone'd come out of something like that disturbed."

Why was it, when you put on a uniform you couldn't talk plain? "Disturbed." That didn't tell you anything more than crazy. Less. If he stopped off at the Seven Spot to cash his check Winnie got disturbed, but that wasn't crazy.

"How come she keeps wanting to go home? That's the *last* place I'd want to be if I was her. I mean, suppose they was waiting for her, what would she want to go back there for? Can you imagine that, keeping her locked up like that, not hardly feeding her or cleaning her up, just to get at her dinky social security?"

Bitzer put on her professional face. "The human mind's strange, Hobie."

That was no answer; any dummy could tell you that.

He looked in on her two or three times during the afternoon, but it was like talking to a wall. Not that she was like Silent Sam; she wasn't that bad at all. Sam, he just sat and stared. You could stick your face right in front of him and scream and he wouldn't blink. At first it was scary, him just staring like that, but after a while you got used to him and he was just part of the room like a chair or a bed. But you couldn't get through to her. No matter what you said, she had just one thing on her mind.

"Can I go home?"

He sat on the edge of her bed and she watched him with immense eyes.

"Can I go home?"

"What do you want to go there for?" She really made you mad after a while. "Look how good you got it here, woman! Good food, people to wait on you hand and foot. Hell, all they wanted was to steal your money, don't you know that?"

It didn't do any good at all.

He stopped in her doorway on his way out. The sun slanted in, drawing a sharp bright yellowish-white square around her chair. Her fingers stroked the chicken. "I'll see you," he said, moving away. He came back.

"Can I go home?" She didn't say it with any hope.

Gently he shifted her out of the bright sunlit square, rolled her into the shadow. So the light wouldn't hurt her eyes.

"You have a good night, hear?" She was so pale, so shrunken up. "We'll talk some more tomorrow. You sleep good, Mrs. Cheney."

He kept thinking about her on the bus and that made him mad, too. You could get as crazy as they were if you dragged them home with you.

After supper he sat with Winona on the small brick patio he'd spent one whole summer putting in and told her about the Chicken Lady. He called her Mrs. Cheney.

Winona shook her head. "That's very sad. But, you know, maybe she figures no matter how they treated her, they needed her."

That was so crazy he didn't want to talk about it anymore. Before he fell asleep he couldn't shake her out of his mind. He kept pushing her away into the shadows and she kept rolling out into a bright square of sunlight, holding her stupid chicken.